# GUILTY!

## AS CHARGED

### by
### P. Alan White

Published & Distributed by:

**EMBRACE
the
CROSS**

*Christian Ministries*
Counseling Division
P.O. Box 6156
Katy, Texas 77491-6156

Printed in the USA by

*M*O**RRIS**
*PUBLISHING*

3212 E. Hwy 30
Kearney, NE 68847
800-650-7888

# ACKNOWLEDGEMENTS

There are many people that have assisted so much in putting this book together, serving as supporters or in a discipleship role and deserve recognition. In fact, I would hate to start naming all of them in fear that someone would be left unnamed. However, there are several organizations that have contributed with this effort and I would like to thank them now.

**ALL PROFITS** from the sale of this book will be divided between these non-profit, Christian ministries for the furtherance of the Gospel of Jesus Christ through their ministries. Your support of these ministries with your purchase and donations is appreciated!

**FOCUS on the FAMILY**
**Dr. James Dobson**
**Colorado Springs, Colorado**

**PRISON FELLOWSHIP MINISTRIES**
**Mr. Charles W. Colson**
**Washington, D.C.**

**TYNDALE Theological Seminary**
**& Biblical Institute**
**Drs. Mal & Lacy Couch**
**Fort Worth, Texas**

This book is dedicated to my
wonderful, loving parents,
who have loved me and stood
by me through everything;


to Carrie Fennell, who
showed me that my actions
affect everyone around me;


to Randy McBride, who has
displayed God's unconditional
love when I needed it most.


I love all of you
very, very much!!

# CONTENTS

# FOREWORD

It isn't easy to be honest about the painful mistakes we make in life. But Alan takes us through detail after detail of errors of pride and circumstances that finally sent him to prison. "Yet Alan was raised in a Christian home," some will say. "How can we learn from his life of mistakes?" Indeed, because of his Christian upbringing, that canvas backdrop of his early life will serve him well in his story of personal recovery!

Alan always wanted to be a policeman. But he ended up in the U.S. Air Force and later the U.S. Marine Corps. From military police work to an embassy assignment in Russia, to The White House in Washington, DC, Alan was given important work that reflected his intelligence and talents. But something was missing!

Admitting he "wanted to impress" others, he used a stolen credit card to purchase clothes that would enhance his image. Step by step, Alan was on the way downhill to deeper problems.

Leaving the military, Alan joined a civilian police department. Again, he was on his way up the ladder in a promising career opportunity. But he was caught stealing a fellow officer's payroll check. "All the rules were broken," he admits. "I destroyed the trust, faith, and confidence which family, friends...had placed in me." This time Alan served time. Coming out of jail, he had lost his wife!

In time, and through more pain and problems, Alan truly finds the Lord Jesus in a genuine personal way. With painful disclosure, he tells how he had to face his Master and himself. He had to realize he had been driven by his desire to impress others and gain material success.

The road to rebuilding trust is a large part of Alan's story. He has done this by traveling a different road of renewed discipline. For example, he reached out for a personal knowledge of God's Word and for the discipline of biblical education. He enrolled as a student at **TYNDALE Theological Seminary.** To help others, he concentrated on Biblical Ministerial Counseling as a major for his MA degree and for the Doctor of Ministry degree he is currently working toward.

In many ways, Alan's story is **OUR** story. We accept Christ as Savior but then too often we test Him. "What can I get away with as a believer in Christ?" we ask. We forget that God will take us through dark valleys in order to cause us to cry out to Him. By whatever means, the Lord is working through our mistakes to conform us to Christ. Alan is an extreme example, but an example nevertheless, of this sometimes painful spiritual journey.

Lacy Couch, MA, D.Min.
Department Head
Biblical Ministerial Counseling Dept.
**TYNDALE Theological Seminary**
Fort Worth, Texas

# PART 1

## GUILTY AS CHARGED:
### The Beginning

# Chapter 1

# *THE BEGINNING*

● ● ● ● ● ● ● ● ● ● ● ● ● ● ● ● ● ● ● ●

*"Agree with thine adversary quickly, while thou art in the way with him; lest at any time the adversary deliver thee to the judge, and the judge deliver thee to the officer and thou be cast into prison."*

*Matthew 5:25*

"Mr. Foreman, has the jury reached a verdict?" 'Yes, your Honor.' "What say ye?" 'We the jury, of the 209th District Court of Houston, Harris County, Texas, find the defendant, Paul Alan White, guilty as charged of the offense of forgery and hereby sentence him to forty years in the Texas Department of Corrections.'

Mary immediately responded, "Your Honor, we would like the jury polled." ' Juror #1, is this your vote?' "Yes"; 'Juror #2, is this your vote?' "Yes"; Juror #3, is this..."

As the judge continued polling each juror, my knees became weak and gave way beneath me. It began to sink in. Forty years...how could I have been so stupid as to pull a stunt like this? Where did I go wrong?

These questions, along with my entire life began to roll in front of my eyes, as if on a large screen TV. In the past thirteen years, I had been arrested between eight and twelve times and sentenced to serve over eighty-eight years in county, state, and federal prisons. I had served close to five years behind bars and was now facing another four to sixteen years.

Why had I committed five felony crimes? Could they have been prevented? When would I learn?

# Chapter 2

# *A SMALL TOWN BEGINNING*

● ● ● ● ● ● ● ● ● ● ● ● ● ● ● ● ● ● ● ●

*"I will say of the Lord, He is my refuge and my fortress; my God; in Him will I trust."*
*Psalms 91:2*

My life began in the small, Northwest Louisiana town of Homer. A former "oil boom" town of 5000 people where everyone knew each other and everything that happens.

I was the youngest of three children born into one of the most loving and Christian families that could ever have been. My father, James, a public school administrator, deacon and Sunday School teacher, was well known and respected throughout the parish. (Louisiana has parishes, not counties) Janie, my mom, worked as an office manager and insurance clerk for one of the two medical clinics in town. I have two brothers, Wayne and Jim. Both excelled in their classes and sports in school and did very well. Jim was selected as an All District, All State and Honorable Mention All American in football with numerous scholarships available to him upon graduation. I admired both of them very much. My maternal grandparents, Rev. and Mrs. E.N. Burns, lived with us as well. PaPa, a retired Baptist preacher, raised me until I started grade school due to mom and dad both working.

My childhood was as normal as any other child from this area. Mom and dad worked very hard to provide for us and I cannot remember ever needing anything while growing up. As I grew older, I held the usual jobs of a teenager. I made and sold hot-pot holders, peddled greeting cards door-to-door, mowed yards, bailed hay and was a lifeguard at the town swimming pool. I also held jobs as a service station attendant and delivery boy for a drug store. During the summers, we would burn-up gasoline driving around town, "rolling yards" with toilet paper or stealing watermelons from the local farmers.

Homer only had one grade school, junior high, and high school until my sophomore year when a private school was established. In a small town such as this, you are bound to have at least some of the same teachers your older siblings had. This unfortunate circumstance happen to me. Unlike my brothers, I was not considered a "sports jock." I did enjoy golf and tennis, but neither were available as organized team sports. Likewise, I never excelled in my studies, barely maintaining a 2.0 GPA. If my school work did not get completed prior to my leaving school for the day, it just did not get done. At this time, I began to hear, "Why can't you be more like your brothers?" This did not come from family, but from teachers and friends. This went on my entire three years of high school.

I received my driver's license in September of my freshman year. In November, I was going to a basketball game some ten miles away and was late due to my scheduled ride not picking me up. I was in such a hurry, it caught the attention of the local state trooper. He informed me that radar had clocked me traveling 83 mph in a 70 mph speed zone. This was prior to the 55 mph law, of course. Since I was a minor, he told me to report, with one or both of my parents, within seven days to the sheriff. I delayed telling mom and dad until the night before we had to see the sheriff. I did not know that they knew about the ticket the night it happen. **(Small Town!)** Sheriff J.R. "Snap" Oakes had known mom and dad since their college days together, so he allowed dad to decide what my punishment would be. Dad took my driver's license for three months.

That was my first "official" introduction to law enforcement, but my second meeting came the next year in high school. I was approached at school by a student and asked if I wanted to buy some "weed" or marijuana. This was new to me and fairly new to Homer. I knew nothing about it and was frankly scared of it. Not wanting anything to do with it, I left school during lunch period and went to the sheriff's office to report it. I gave them the student's name and he was later arrested at school.

I really disliked school and had made the decision to enter the military once school was completed. The U.S. Air Force recruiter was the first to visit our school that year, so I enlisted in the delayed enlistment program in February prior to my May graduation. The past few years had given me the career field I would have for several years to come; law enforcement.

Entry into the U.S. Air Force came just three days after graduation in the field of security police, with additional training as a patrol dog (K-9) handler, as my assigned duty. I really loved the work, especially working with the dogs, but the Air Force lacked discipline, which I very much needed and wanted. It was nothing more than an "8 to 5" job where everyone dressed alike. After six months, I applied for and received an inter-service transfer to the U.S. Marine Corps.

# Chapter 3

# WEST MEETS EAST

● ● ● ● ● ● ● ● ● ● ● ● ● ● ● ● ● ● ●

*"For if a man think himself to be something, when he is nothing, he deceiveth himself."*

*Galatians 6:3*

Entering the marines, I requested to go into the Military Police (MP) field but the Marine Corps required you to be twenty-one years old and I was only eighteen. My test scores were high in other areas, so I was placed in the aviation maintenance field.

After completing basic training, again, I was assigned to the Naval Air Station-Memphis to train as a structure mechanic or metalsmith. In the corps, anytime you enter a school, they ask you to complete your "dream sheet" stating where you would like to be assigned after training. Most of the time you were only dreaming to get your choice, thus it's name. My first choice was to be assigned to HMX-1, the Presidential Helicopter Squadron, Executive Flight Detachment outside Washington, DC, however, I was sent to VMGR-252 at Marine Corps Air Station-Cherry Point, NC to work on the KC-130 aircraft. (so much for dream sheets) The C-130 is the largest aircraft within the Marine Corps inventory and is used as an inflight refueler, (flying gas station), for other aircraft and as a troop/cargo transport. It did not take long for me to see I did not want to be on the grease-monkey end of aviation; I wanted to fly. A request was made and permission granted for me to train as a flight engineer and crew member where I began logging over 2200 flight hours on the C-130. I also received my second meritorious promotion.

Everything at this point was great!! I was flying all over the United States and the Atlantic including Bermuda, the Azore

Islands, Portugal and Puerto Rico; I had two early zone promotions and I was no longer hearing, "Why can't you be like your brothers?" Alan was doing just fine on his own with help from no one else. But something was missing...there was no real happiness in my life.

One day a group of recruiters were on base looking for "a few good men" volunteers to be assigned to the Marine Security Guard School in Washington, DC. This sounded exciting to me; being in the nation's capitol where the heart of government and military existed. It was also back in the security field.

The Marine Corps has the distinct honor of being selected and trained by the U.S. Department of State to guard our embassies and consulates around the world. They also guard The White House, fly the president and staff aboard the green and white helicopters seen on TV and the Marine Corps Band, **"The President's Own"**, is the official band of The White House.

The grass always looks greener on the other side, so I volunteered to go. After some two months, notification was received that I had been selected provided I made a three year extension on my military enlistment.

Embassy school was an eight week program with training in foreign relations and protocol, photography, language training for your country of assignment, security procedures including locks, safes, and the destruction of classified documents, along with martial arts and special weapons training. More than 220 men began training in my class with only 130 completing. It was a very rigid course and many failed to make the grades, pass the personal inspections or could not obtain a Top Secret security clearance as required. I finished eighth in my class and received my first choice of assignment from the dream sheet. I was headed to the American Embassy, Moscow, USSR, where I would be assigned to internal security of the embassy and to the Personal Protection Unit (PPU) of the ambassador. I was also the only one to request Russia.

It took some six weeks, after completion of school, for the Soviet Embassy in Washington to approve my visa application. During this wait, I went back to Homer for thirty days leave, as I was told it may be several years before coming home again. While on this leave, I committed my first crime. I had a friend drive me to the airport to go back to Washington. He dropped one of his dad's credit cards on the floor, I picked it up, put it in my pocket and never told him. The State Department had given us $300 to purchase clothes for the assignment, but I had spent over $150 just for an overcoat. Wanting to impress others with what I had, I used the card in the DC area to buy additional clothes. No identification was asked for when the purchases were made, and I did not think it would be traced to me, but it was...all the way to Moscow. My friend's dad refused to press charges provided restitution was made on the purchases.

My assignment to Moscow was highlighted by several events. During my stay here, I traveled with Ambassador Walter J. Stoessal on his trips around Moscow and throughout Europe. I worked with the Secret Service to provide security for the SALT II talks with Secretary of State Henry Kissinger and Soviet President Leonid Brezhnev and we were the victims of the bombardment of the embassy with microwave radiation. The Soviets claimed this was to re-charge the batteries on their listening devices or "bugs" in the building. We also had two bomb scares. Over the next few months, I traveled to every European country except Czechoslovakia. All of this at the age of twenty.

As exciting as it was, being in the Soviet Union did have many drawbacks. McDonald's had not yet arrived and "fast food" was unknown to the Soviets. If you wanted to eat out, reservations had to be made three to four days ahead and we were only allowed to go to four different restaurants, where we <u>always</u> had the same tables! The tables and flowers were "wired for sound!" If you got to the restaurant by 6:00 pm, you were lucky to be out by 11:00 pm. The Soviets, like most of Europe, do not get in a hurry to eat. It is an all-night affair for them. You could not go out for dinner **AND** go to the ballet the same night. There was just not enough time.

Not only were the tables and flowers wired, so was your own apartment and telephone. While re-wiring an electrical outlet in my apartment, I found a "bug" in the box with the outlet. Once while using the phone, I completed a conversation and hung-up the receiver. As soon as I did, I remembered something else that I needed to tell that person, so I picked up the receiver to call them back. When I did, I heard the conversation I had just had being replayed. That's how I found out about their bugs. There was no place you could go and talk without being recorded.

Soviet dry cleaning also lacked a lot to be desired. It consisted of "dipping" your suits and uniforms in lighter fluid or kerosene, then allowing them to dry while being pressed. Wear your slacks for a hour or so and your legs were burning and you had a rash. Don't even think about lighting a match!! Sometime later, we began to send our clothes to Helsinki, Finland for cleaning.

We also had to order our milk from Helsinki...three weeks in advance. This was a quick lesson in "menu planning" for a young bachelor. Once every four months, we also received a plane of supplies and food from Germany. It was so good to get the little things we take for granted here; like "Imperial Sugar." All we could get there was raw sugar. How about "Tabasco Sauce" or lettuce for a salad. We only got this when the plane came in.

The cultural events in Moscow were excellent though. I became a big fan of the Bolshoi Ballet Company while there, seeing them perform **"Swan Lake"** over fifty times and **"The Nutcracker"** over thirty times. The Pulshkin and the Kremlin Museums held the most beautiful pieces of art, icons, and samovars ever seen. I had obtained several icons and prerevolutionary samovars from the under ground black market to send home, but they never made it out of the country when my personal property was shipped from Moscow.

Last, but not least, we were privileged to be followed by the Komitet Gosudarstvennoi Bezopasnasti (or KGB for short), every time we left the compound. It was funny at first because we ran three miles a day; rain, sleet or snow. Many times I would have to stop and wait for "my agents" to catch up with me, then resume my run. You did not want them to think you were trying to get away from them and go somewhere else. They were in very poor condition to have been assigned to one of the marines there, but we were really no threat to them. They were just doing their job and we were doing ours. Sometime later, I learned Alex and Petrov's names and even though you could not call us friends, we did talk. I would tell them my route in case they got too far behind. I also gave them a case of American vodka on New Years of 1976 (and also helped them drink it). They enjoyed it much more than Soviet vodka as it was 180 proof alcohol.

To help me mentally deal with the hassle of Soviet life, I felt it was getting back at them by buying and selling on the black market, as stated earlier. And believe me, there <u>was</u> a market!! Levi jeans sold for $300 a pair; $475 if you had the jacket to go with them. Albums from the west sold for $50 each regardless of artist and our 1¢ "Super Bubble" bubble gum went for $5 a piece. A friend on embassy duty, in Germany, would send my "goods" in the diplomatic pouch by a courier so the Soviets would not intercept it in shipping.

The Soviet currency, the ruble, was worth 32¢ on the international exchange market during 1975-76, and it was illegal to import or export rubles. As embassy employees, we were charged $1.48 US for $1.00 Soviet. I began buying rubles, on the black market, at the rate of $7 Soviet for $1 US. They would then be sold to other embassy employees at the rate of $5 Soviet for $1 US. Everyone was happy...the black market people because they now had "hard" currency; embassy staff because they were getting a great deal; and me, who was still making a profit. The only unhappy people were the Soviet government officials who lost their profit from the $1.48 rate they had been charging.

My small enterprise did not last too long and neither did I. After eating so many times at a wired table, having my phone calls tapes, and being followed everywhere I went, it began to get to me. I became very paranoid. I fell into the role play of a cold war spy; like James Bond, Agent 007. I never achieved "007" status. I lost it somewhere around "005½." I began to do things I should not. I enlisted my Soviet contacts on the black market to get any kind of information they could, for a price. I wanted access to buildings and areas I should never get caught in. If caught, the embassy would have denied even knowing I was in the Soviet Union, much less working at the embassy. The risks being taken got larger and larger. My photography had placed me into trouble several times, but in my mind, it was all for my country. The embassy never complained to me about the quality of my work; only that I was real close to being caught by the Soviets. None of the things I was doing were my assigned job. Some of these are still classified after more than 18 years with yet others being declassified many years past. I have a slide program that is shown to groups in regards to my stay in Russia using some of the declassified pictures taken there. I fell deeper and deeper into my role playing. So deep in fact, that I had to be extracted and hospitalized in Germany. After some three weeks there, it seem to get worse. Everyone I saw: doctors, nurses, friends, even my commanding officer for Europe were perceived, by me, as KGB sent to kill me. I tried to escape "my captors" and sedated, I fell down two flights of stairs, ran into walls, doors, and finally tried to jump from a third floor window to prevent being captured by them. The glass cut my forehead and left eye but the window had a metal screen on the outside that prevented my fall. Thank God, because I would be dead now if not for that. It took over twenty stitches over my eye and forehead. That same wound has now been reopened over five times and the scar tissue will no longer hold stitches. They put me into a straight-jacket, strapped me in bed, and sedated me even more until a flight back to the states could be arranged. The doctors refused to remove the jacket on the plane, even to use the rest room. The last hour of the flight, I had to lie in my waste on the stretcher. Upon arrival in the states, I was admitted into the U.S. Naval Hospital in Portsmouth, VA. They took one look at the file and set-up another flight, the same day, to the U.S. Naval Hospital in Bethesda, MD.

Only limited contact with other patients and staff was allowed for over two weeks. The staff was somewhat afraid that I may be in danger until they could research and check the story in the case file. I was kept in a secure area of the hospital until everyone; including doctors, State Department, Marine Corps, Central Intelligence, and Defense Intelligence was sure I was not being tracked or followed.

My girlfriend was flying in from Moscow to see me the week of July fourth. The hospital denied my request for a weekend pass, due to security reasons, so I went AWOL (absent without leave). Vicki was from Seattle, assigned to the Economic Section of the embassy, and we had been dating since we met at the State Department during my stay there for school. After my posting to Moscow, she requested a transfer as well. The marines were prohibited from fraternizing with the Soviets for any reason, outside of official duty. Several marines were charged with violating this regulation in the mid-1980's. I came back to the hospital on Monday morning, but the hospital had filed charges against me for being AWOL and the doctors had given their diagnosis of me as a "paranoid schizophrenic with an anti-social personality" with the suggestion that I be discharged from the military.

When released from the hospital, I was told to report to my commanding officer at headquarters. He had the charge sheet of my being AWOL and wanted to hear my explanation. I told him the situation with the hospital and that I just wanted some time with Vicki. He asked if I regretted going AWOL and I told him, "No sir, and if I thought that was the only way to get to see her, I would do it again." He tore up the charge sheet. After reading the doctors recommendation for discharge, he said, "Hogwash!! You have an outstanding record. In over three years you have no problems at all, you have two early promotions, you are flight qualified, scuba qualified, PPU certified, and you were in the top ten of your class. Go select where you would like to go on your next assignment."

While awaiting orders to my next post, I had requested Dublin, Ireland, I was assigned to The White House Security Detachment and to HMX-1, the Presidential Helicopter Squadron. This was during President Gerald Ford's term in office.

After some six months of waiting for my Dublin assignment to commence, I felt my career in the Marine Corps was over with this information in my medical file...and it was. My re-posting had been denied at HQMC by a medical review board and I was to be discharged as a sergeant, E-5, after three years and seven months with an Honorable Discharge.

---

*Excerpts from **"Behind the Iron Curtain"**, also by the author, are included in this chapter. © 1981 Texas Professional Photographer used by permission.

Page 10 – THE GUARDIAN JOURNAL – Thurs., Dec. 18, 1975

## Paul White Gets Assignment To Russia

The Department of State Office of Security has announced the assignment of Paul White to the state's Foreign Service Branch. White is the son of Mr. and Mrs. J. O. White of Homer, and a 1973 graduate of Homer High School.

He has been assigned to the Personal Protection Service Unit to the Ambassador at the American Embassy in Moscow, USSR.

While attending eight weeks of school in Washington, White received training in security regulations, destruction of classified material; foreign service establishments, contact with foreign nationals and special training with all types of weapons.

GUILTY AS CHARGED

American Embassy, Moscow, USSR
January 1976

GUILTY AS CHARGED

# Chapter 4

# *LIFE AFTER RUSSIA*

• • • • • • • • • • • • • • • • • • • •

*"He that covereth his sins shall not prosper; but whoso confesseth and forsaketh them shall have mercy."*

*Proverbs 28:13*

I had always had a desire to work in law enforcement and my military assignments only re-enforced this desire. I feel it may have been because my paternal grandfather had been a police officer until he was killed in the line of duty. I never got to meet him.

Between the time I was told of a discharge and the actual time released, I was in contact with a small police department about 14 miles north of Hot Springs, Arkansas. After my release from the Marine Corps, I was hired within a month. The chief there was a retired Air Force master-sergeant in the security police field and he was impressed with the training I had received, especially the PPU certification and K-9 school.

This was an unusual department. It was a state certified police department, but we were also commissioned deputies for two different counties. The reason for this; it was the police department for a master-planned retirement community, Hot Springs Village, which is located in Garland and Saline Counties. This was okay for awhile, but it was more of a public relations job than it was law enforcement.

Out of the twelve officers on the department, I was the youngest and the only one living within the boundaries of HSV. One Saturday afternoon, while off duty, I came upon a motorcycle accident where a twelve-year old girl had been injured. She had been thrown from the motorcycle, landed on a rock and cut her eye lid to the point it was barely attached. Knowing the department only had two officers on duty at the time, I administered first aid, put her in my car, and drove her and her sister to the nearest hospital, fourteen miles away. The chief called me in on Monday morning and said this had been an unauthorized action and I was suspended, without pay, for three days. After the three days, he said he did not think I was going to "fit in" with their little group and asked for my resignation.

At this time, I went to work for a cable TV company installing cable for the homes in HSV. It was also at this point that I married a wonderful young lady I had met there, Joanna Eaton. We had known each other for about a year, meeting when I left the marines. I did not like the cable job, so I applied and was accepted to the Shreveport Police Department in Louisiana, about fifty miles from my hometown of Homer.

I completed the academy fourth in my class of thirty-five. My military training had, once again, given me a slight edge in certain areas of the academy. I was even asked to teach first aid, CPR and emergency procedures to the new academy cadet classes. I was now back where I wanted to be: law enforcement.

I was very fortunate to be assigned to work with a training officer who was very easy to work with and had years of experience on the streets. We got along well together. Ricky Walker and his wife, Cissy, Joanna and I quickly became close friends and got together to cook-out, play cards or just visit. Ricky and I worked the 2-10 pm shift, so dinner with the wives did not occur too often. Although, Cissy was a police dispatcher and I would often see her more than I would Joanna.

After several weeks on the streets, Ricky and I received a call of someone trying to pass counterfeit money to a drive-in bank. We arrived, with two other units, and took the suspect into custody. Four or five of the officers were trying to figure out which bills were "bogus." Ricky asked me what I thought and I pointed out the fake bills while they were still in his hands. He asked, "How do you know?" I told him they were cut too small and the ink color was off. After I had the bills in my hands, I pointed out several other things wrong with them. The Secret Service had taught me this when I worked with them in Moscow. I now had the respect of my training officer.

Some six months into the job, I went to the watch commander's desk to pick up my check. All the checks were in one bundle and you just went through them until you found your check. I got mine, complained as usual, and put it into my pocket. My complaint was that I was making $200 a month less than told I would before moving from Arkansas. It was not until the next day that I realized another officer's check was with mine.

Joanna and I had just bought a second car because her job took her the opposite direction from mine. We were also paying fifty percent of her salary to the employment agency that found her the job. As a lot of newlywed couples are, we were over extended. Whether for these reasons or others, I still do not know, but I gave into the temptation, forged the officer's signature, and cashed the check with mine. By going to a branch of my bank that I normally did not go to and being on duty and in uniform, the bank seldom asked for additional identification. They just assumed the other check was my partner's, who they could see sitting in the car. The chance of getting caught, I felt, was slim.

I can always claim the excuses above and others for why this was done, but they are only excuses, not valid reasons. It is also not taking responsibility for my actions. In the past, I never had anyway. I had always blamed someone or something for my problems; never myself. All of this does not change the fact that what I did was wrong; not only legally, but morally. It would have been so easy to take the check back the next day and explain what happen. All the rules were broken that I had been taught by so many while growing up. I destroyed the trust, faith, and confidence which family, friends, fellow officers, and the community had placed in me. This was done, not once, but twice. It was this second time that got me. I could now hear, "Why can't you be more like your brothers", only this time, it was me saying it.

I was arrested, charged with one count of felony forgery, one count of felony theft, convicted and sentenced to serve twenty-five years in the Louisiana State Penitentiary at Angola. After serving nine months at the Caddo Parish Jail, assigned as a trusty at the sheriff's academy working on their patrol cars, the judge brought me back into court and suspended the remaining sentence. He knew what would happen to an ex-cop in Angola or any other prison. He did not give me justice; he gave his mercy!!

It was now time to start over; in a different town, a new career field and without Joanna. I was now divorced.

**GUILTY AS CHARGED**

# Policeman Arrested in Payroll Theft

A 22-year-old Shreveport policeman was arrested Tuesday afternoon and booked into city jail on a charge of forgery in connection with the alleged theft of two police payroll checks.

Patrolman Paul Allen White of 7000 Fern Ave., Apt. 89, was booked at 3 p.m. and later transferred to the Caddo Parish jail. He has reportedly been fired from the police force.

Also, a city hall porter, Paul Fredieu, 22, of 1817 Perrin St. was arrested July 21 and booked on a charge of forgery in connection with the theft of one of the checks.

The arrest stems from the alleged theft of the checks from the patrol desk area. Police said the first check was reported missing June 15 and the second one month later.

An investigation was begun after it was deteremined the first check had indeed been stolen and not lost. A local bank reportedly returned the cashed check to police, and Fredieu was arrested after his signature was matched with the one on the check.

The bank returned the second check to the Caddo Parish District Attorney's office after it was also cashed. Investigators obtained handwriting samples from White after the second check was stolen and later matched them with the signature on the payroll check.

At the time the checks were stolen they were placed in a stack at the booking desk and officers got their own check. The checks are not distributed by the watch commander.

Release bond for White, who had been employed as a patrolman six months, has been set at $2,014.

GUILTY AS CHARGED

# Chapter 5

# *TAKE NOTHING BUT PICTURES...*

● ● ● ● ● ● ● ● ● ● ● ● ● ● ● ● ● ● ●

*"Love not the world, neither the things that are in the world. If any man love the world, the love of the Father is not in him."*

1 John 2:15

As mentioned earlier, Uncle Sam taught me photography as part of my embassy training. I decided to give this a try as I moved back to Hot Springs.

Having lived here before, there were several friends that really helped me now. When first moving to Hot Springs, Doug & Sarita Cox had taken me into their extended family where we became very close. Doug had once been a Memphis police officer and had tried to talk me out of law enforcement as a career. How I wished I had taken his advise.

Doug & Sarita owned a gift shop in town and asked me to photograph different locations for use as post cards. I also began to photograph weddings and parties. A desire to open my own studio formed but I lacked the money to purchase equipment. I answered an ad in the newspaper for a portrait photographer working with Olan Mills Studios and was hired to work in East and Southeast Texas as a road photographer. I would go into a hotel and set-up a mobile studio from one day to three weeks. I was also contracting weddings from my Olan Mills clients.

After a year with Olan Mills, I had the money needed for my studio and opened **The Image Studio** in Richmond, Texas. It was a very successful start-up studio in a town of 15-20,000 people where three other studios already existed.

I had decided to limit my work to executive portraiture and weddings and within six to eight months, our work was being submitted in portrait competitions with awards on the state and national level being won for the wedding work. The ninth month open, I was named International Wedding Photographer of the Month by Wedding Photographers International of Santa Monica, California. After the announcement, my wedding bookings jumped from ten for a three month period to over thirty-five for the same period.

I had previously restricted work to the tri-county area around Richmond, but we now found ourselves traveling all over Texas, Louisiana, Arkansas, and New Mexico. Some people were planning their wedding date and time around our availability. One three-day weekend, we had nine weddings with five on one day.

We started with a sunrise service on the beach in Galveston, followed by a 10 am in Richmond, a 1 pm in Rosenberg, a 3 pm in Richmond, and a 7 pm in Bay City. It was policy not to schedule a wedding if I could not personally photograph the ceremony. Many people liked to be assured that someone they had not met would be arriving to photograph their wedding. This really helped in our success. On all of the weddings, I would photograph the ceremony and formal portraits and assistants would handle the receptions while I traveled to the next wedding. They would then follow me to the next location. That one day, we traveled a combined 1060 miles, used ninety rolls of film (over 2160 pictures), wore three tuxedos, six shirts, and had a twenty-hour work day. It was some of our best work!

We started doing underwater photography since I had resumed scuba diving. Wall murals would be made of underwater scenes and later be sold to interior decorators. They loved them and bought all we could come up with.

Alan was back on top!! Everything was going my way. Traveling across the United States and the Caribbean, the money was good, and I was well known in the area. Perhaps this success came along because clients were never told of my law enforcement career, arrest, and prison time. They did know about my time in Russia because some of the pictures taken there were displayed in the studio. It seemed to add to my credibility as a photographer. However, all this publicity, notoriety of my work, and success did no good. I was not happy and I needed a change.

## Chapter 6

# *AN UNDER SEA ADVENTURE*

● ● ● ● ● ● ● ● ● ● ● ● ● ● ● ● ● ● ●

*"Let your character be free from the love of money, being satisfied with your present circumstances; for He Himself said, 'I will not in anyway fail you nor give you up nor leave you without support. I will not forsake you."*

*Hebrews 13:5 (Amp.)*

Some of you may remember a TV series entitled "Sea Hunt" starring Lloyd Bridges. If you do not, it was a 1960's series where Bridges played the part of a scuba diver. It was this show that first sparked my interest in the underworld of the sea.

Taking advantage of the opportunity in the military to learn this skill, I then re-entered diving while in photography. I grew to the point in my diving, that all I wanted to do was dive. My love for this sport grew and grew until I wanted to share this joy with others. If you have never been diving in a body of water like the Caribbean, the West Indies, the Mediterranean or South America, then you do not know what you are missing. In my opinion, the sights underwater far surpass the ones above water. I began to work for a dive shop in Houston to earn my advanced ratings needed to teach. It was here that I fell to crime once more.

Traveling extensively to Mexico, the Cayman Islands, Belize, Jamacia and South America, I was over extended on my credit cards. I was told by several companies to cut them up and return them to the issuing company. I did not. I knew the resorts were one to three months behind on receiving the "hot card" alert bulletins, if they received them at all, so I kept using, my cards. This was nothing more than a deliberate attempt to defraud the credit card companies. All of my expenses; air travel, meals, and hotel were covered by the company yet, I charged between $6000-9000 on alcohol, marijuana (that I didn't want anything to do with in Homer), parties, and "junk" while on trips. We would go to clubs to dance and drink and when the night was over, I would pick up the tab for everyone. There was one trip to Jamaica where four of us had a bar bill of over $970 for five days. You might say I was trying to "buy" my friends.

It was about this time the store gave a party for our clients. When one lady was ready to leave, it was discovered that her car had been stolen form the parking lot. As we called the police, she pulled out her wallet to get her car registration and license numbers. I later saw her wallet and credit cards on the table and took several of them. They were used to charge over $1000 worth of goods the following two days. Kristi, I really wish I knew where you are to say how sorry I am.

I was arrested and charged with two counts of credit card abuse; one on her cards and one on my own. Texas was unaware of my Louisiana conviction and I lied to them when they asked, so I was treated as a first time offender. Judge Woody Densen, of the 248th District Court, sentenced me to six years deferred adjudication and to make full restitution on the card charges. This was a form of probation that, should I remain clear of trouble for six years, the charge would not be on my record. Judge Densen was also a diver and he gave his permission for me to continue traveling outside the U.S. on trips. The only problem was, I no longer had a job.

This was around the time of the civil unrest in El Salvador in Central America. I had kept in touch with two former marines that still worked for the government, and as we talked one day, they asked if I might be interested in doing some contract work for them. With my military background and the more recent work experience as a dive instructor, I was to travel to Central America a few times a month on the pretense of "being on a dive trip." Since I was unemployed and owed the court between $8000-9000, why not? It was not until some time later that I found out the government likes to have, what they call, "plausible deniability" when they conduct certain operations. I fit right into their requirements for this; a two-time convicted felon and currently on probation. There would be no way someone would consider me to be working for the U.S. Government should I ever get caught doing something or being somewhere I should not. This continued for ten months until I was no longer needed. I never saw that what I did was ever needed or even useful but, it paid my court debt in full within six months, which made my probation officer very happy. When seeing this, he told me even though I would be on probation for five more years, I would no longer have to report in to him.

When this job was completed, they failed to ask for my ID card, so I kept it. It would be shown to people to try and impress them as to what I did for a living. I had fallen back into my role playing once again. My stories were a little hard for some people to believe and I had now displayed the card to one too many people. Trying to impress a young lady and to obtain a date with her, I showed the card to her. Little did I know that she was a FBI agent. When she checked with the agency in question, she found out I was no longer employed with them.

Upon returning home from my current job of remodeling /construction one day, I unlocked my door only to be arrested by the FBI before I could get inside and I was charged with impersonating a federal employee. It was ironic at the time because I was working for a company that was remodeling the offices of the FBI in the federal building and they did not realize it. They had been watching my apartment for a few weeks to learn my schedule and they could have picked me up without leaving their office. I was also driving a rental car that was weeks late being turned in and was now charged with auto theft. This charge was later dismissed because it was rented to me; it was just late getting returned.

I was sentenced in the Southern District of Texas Federal Court, Galveston by Judge Hugh Gibson for impersonation and sent to the Federal Correction Institute in Big Spring, Texas, for one year. I was currently in college and Judge Gibson allowed me to complete the term. He told me to turn myself in to the prison in two months. My probation on credit card abuse was now revoked and Judge Densen sentenced me to serve two years in the Texas Department of Corrections, but allowed that sentence to run concurrent with the federal sentence at Big Spring.

**GUILTY AS CHARGED**

FCI Big Spring was known as "Club Fed." It was a minimum security unit that did not have a fence around it. You just promised not to run off. I was first assigned to work in the landscape department. In other words, I cut grass for 30¢ a hour.

Later, a move to the commissary, or prison store for inmates, making 65¢ a hour, was a promotion. This really wasn't punishment. Sure, you lost your freedom to come and go as you pleased, but that was about the only drawback.

We were housed in two-man rooms of the bachelor officer quarters on the old Webb Air Force Base. We had tennis courts, racquetball courts, a complete gym with weight room and sauna, a ¼ mile track, softball field and basketball gym. There were telephones in the dorms along with soda and candy machines. We even had a swimming pool, though I never saw water in it during my stay there.

Big Spring did have some redeeming qualities about it. We held basketball, volleyball, and softball games with the local towns people where the admission and concession monies were given to the United Way. We also donated the money raised from the sell of our soft drink cans to the retirement home across the street. Several nights a week, a few of the men would take their musical instruments over, play and sing for them as well.

The town and prison worked well together and had a very good relationship with each other. The annual disaster drill for Big Spring EMS was held on the grounds of the unit also, with the inmates being the "victims" of the disaster. Most of this has now changed, as FCI Big Spring was upgraded to a medium security unit in 1990 and installed a fence.

Young people, it must be expressed at this point, jails and prisons are not like Big Spring was when I was there. If you have never been exposed to prison life, believe me, you do not want to be. You could not believe everything that goes on behind the walls of a prison. It is not my desire to get into a lot of prison "war stories", but it must be told that this is no game you want to play.

People in prison play for keeps. I have seen men clubbed to death with a 2x4, beat senseless from someone swinging a padlock on a belt, eyes gouged out with ink pens, stomachs cut open and left on the floor by a piece of glass or maybe a "shank" (that is a homemade knife of some kind). I have seen men die from aids in the prime of their lives and of old age. I was once on a unit where over 65% of the population were active homosexuals and many kids were "turned" once they arrived there. Some had no choice. They were weak and could not resist, fight back or protect themselves. Others might borrow items such as coffee, tobacco or candy and then would not be able to repay the items. It would either be "to marry" and perform sex acts or die. Some men would even "sell" their wives to settle up gambling debts. I was stabbed over a piece of chicken, burned with a hot iron, scalded with boiling water and had two slight heart attacks during my first four and a half years behind bars. I was blessed. Others have not been. There have been over thirty men carried out of prison in body bags that I have seen.

This is **NO GAME!** This is for real. You can die in prison over a $2.25 bag of coffee; some have died for less. Someone may wake up one morning and decide they do not like the way you looked at them. That is all it will take.

Prison has taught me several things I will never forget. One is that I am no better than anyone else and worse than many in some areas of my life. Jobs that, at one time, I thought were below me, I now do to be a servant to others. I am not too good to do these things as I had thought. I have also learned patience. I have always been in a hurry in whatever I did or for whatever I wanted. I was not willing to wait. Third, and very important, prison has taught me that I do not want to return!!

Upon leaving Big Spring nine months later, I felt a big change was needed. Not only would I enter a new career field, but for several reasons, my name was changed. One of them was to give me a new start in life without a criminal record. The only problem with this; it only changed my name, not the real person inside.

**GUILTY AS CHARGED**

# Chapter 7

# *FLYING HIGH*

● ● ● ● ● ● ● ● ● ● ● ● ● ● ● ● ● ● ● ● ●

*"...but they that wait upon the Lord shall renew their strength; they shall mount up with wings as eagles; they shall run, and not be weary; and they shall walk, and not faint."*

*Isaiah 40:31*

The only area of my military training that had not been used by now was aviation. I really enjoyed flying and began working to complete my civilian ratings as a commercial pilot. As of today, my experience includes flight time on twenty-seven different type aircraft with a combined 5200 hours flight time. I also received my ratings as a certified ground and flight instructor. My love for flying is just under that of scuba diving.

I started flying freight and cargo for a company in Denver and later moved into corporate aviation. In March 1987, a job with a flight school in Houston, as manager and ground instructor, was offered and accepted. Three months later, a promotion to Director of Operations came where I over-saw seven flight instructors, maintenance operations on 14 aircraft, all courses of instruction, along with keeping the daily books, making deposits, and preparing the payroll/tax reports for the company. I was also traveling to the University of Southern California for additional training in aviation safety and accident investigation.

My desire was to open a business conducting aviation safety inspections for private and corporate flight departments, and accident investigations for insurance companies and legal firms. I had conducted several investigations for small aircraft accidents in the Houston area, was involved with four major airline crash investigations and was hired to conduct a safety survey for the Brazilian Ministry of Aeronautics in Rio de Janiero. I needed to expand my services, but money was needed to do so and to complete my training program with USC. Where would I get this kind of money? My credit was destroyed with the credit card conviction and I had no savings to fall back on.

As manager of the flight school, access to the daily receipts and bank deposits were available to me. Money was taken and adjustments made to the books to cover it up. After a period of time, I began to get restless to expand. Some checks made out to the flight school were deposited into my business account and I left for a two-week school at USC. The bank caught this and notified the flight school. When I returned from school, two of my students, who were also Houston police officers, were waiting for me when I got off the plane at mid-night.

With me gone for two weeks, they had built their case against me and I was charged with theft/embezzlement of $1000. Conviction number four brought a twenty year sentence from Judge Doug Shaver in the 262nd District Court. I was now #501966 in the Texas State Penitentiary.

Due to prison over-crowding and the good-time policy in Texas, I served twenty-four months and was released to serve the remainder of my sentence on parole. My self-talk said I was through with crime and to get my life straight. Besides, I was no good as a crook; I always got caught.

# Chapter 8

# FREE AT LAST

● ● ● ● ● ● ● ● ● ● ● ● ● ● ● ● ● ● ●

*"For we must all appear and be revealed as we are before the judgment seat of Christ, so that each one may receive his pay according to what he has done in the body, whether good or evil."*

*2 Corinthians 5:10 (Amp.)*

About six months prior to my release, a real void was felt in my life. This same feeling occurred every time that I got restless in my jobs. It was an emptiness that could not be explained. At the same time, I began to be aware of the little things around me that had been taken for granted. All of us do this at times. You tend not to appreciate what you have until you no longer have them. Things like flowers blooming, birds singing, green grass and trees, even five minutes of peace and quiet. You see, in prison it is very hard to find these things. Every time you go to the rest room or take a shower, you do so with 30-40 others watching you. Even something as small as a glass of ice water had me craving, as I went eight months without this one time.

A search was begun - - a search back to the roots of my upbringing. Lessons taught by Mom and Dad, PaPa, my minister, and teachers at church while growing up. Even though I had accepted Jesus Christ as my savior when twelve-years old and surrendered to preach at age sixteen, I realized I had never made Christ Lord of my life. I began to have feelings I had never known before and started writing these feelings down in the form of a poem, **"Thoughts After Two Years Gone"** and others. (see appendix)

When my release came, I became active in a wonderful church the following Sunday. This was the most unusual singles department I had ever seen, in that the ages of people ranged from 23-60. Every class I had been in prior to this was divided by ages more closely together. It was this diversity of people that made the class very special to me. They will always have a special place in my heart.

Two things were on my mind. First, I wanted to re-open my aviation safety office. I could no longer testify at trials due to the recent conviction, but I could conduct the investigations. I had even done some work on cases for a law firm while in prison. Second, even though the decision was made to turn my life around, I was not ready to "come clean" with the people I met. I did not trust them to accept me since I had been in prison. It would have been much better to tell them the truth and let them decide for themselves, but I did not give them that choice. A "new and improved" past life was made up to tell them.

An honest effort was made to find a job after my release where application was made to fast-food restaurants, grocery stores, and everywhere else I thought I may be able to find work. Over twenty-five applications were made the first week alone. Most all of them asked if you had ever been convicted of a felony and my answer was yes. I now had twenty-five rejections. No job, no money!! You do not have to tell me how hard jobs are to find, I know. Even for people without criminal records. If given the choice, I too, would have chosen someone else.

After a month of applying and getting turned down, I began working for a lady I had met a few years back. As we became friends, she asked me to help her out in her business until mine got going. My job was doing work preparations for her, training her employees on policy and procedures, helping to set-up new offices, and keeping her books on payroll and accounts payable.

Two years prior, she had shared office space with another company. When this company went out of business, they left their office furniture with her and I found that company's old check book in a file drawer one day. Knowing the company was closed, temptation hit me again, hard! I took seven or eight checks from the old book and began buying supplies and equipment needed to reopen my company. These purchases amounted to over

$2300. I had even been taking money from her for over three months, which amounted to close to $1000, and had adjusted the books to cover it. Here I claimed to care about this woman, yet I was stealing from her at the same time. On top of that, the role playing was still going forward. She knew nothing of my past except for the lies that I had told her. Lies with just enough truth to make them believable, yet even the truth stopped.

A month prior to writing the checks, I was the most miserable person alive. My presence was making the staff miserable as well. They hated to see me come in the door. One of the employees stated, "Alan looks like a picture of doom. He has this black cloud over his head every time he walks in the door." The sad part was, I did.

I was upset my business was not going forward and at the same time, the Lord was dealing with me over what I had done. The problem was, I did not realize this at the time.

Samantha* knew something was wrong, but assumed it was due to my business or lack of it. Sam is a very strong Christian the Lord was now using in my life. He knew I would listen to her and He gave her a love for me unlike no other, just so she could help me and deal with me. Most anyone else would have told me to take a hike...over the Grand Canyon!

I was now at the breaking point; mentally, as well as physically. Sam confronted me and I told her what had been done. Not my past; just the check issue. She did not find out about my past until later in court. Sam had been to church with me on several occasions and knew my teacher. After speaking with her over the week-end, she felt I should speak to him and seek his counsel on the situation.

Doug Rimmer is one of the strongest Christian men that I have ever had the pleasure of meeting. We have had our rough spots to overcome because Doug made me take a long, deep look at myself and I did not like this in the least. Doug has had an impact on my life that I may never be able to express in words. Doug is also a U.S. Customs officer. As usual, Sam was right!

Doug and I met after church for almost four hours. I told him about what I had done, how I felt that I could not go back to prison, and how I just could not go on any longer...I was considering suicide. We prayed, cried, and talked some more. After we had lunch, we called two lawyers that he knew and spoke with them. Neither were in criminal law, but we all decided the best thing to do was turn myself in and confess to the crime.

That night, Sam and I went to **The Bread of Life** church in Houston where Bro. Dusty Kemp was preaching from 2 Corinthians 5:10 on accountability; of what we do and having to answer for our actions in heaven. Dusty must have known about me being there because he spoke directly to me the whole night. At least it felt like it. It was a wonder that I heard a single word he said, because I cried the entire service.

Sam and Doug agreed to go with me the next day to see my parole officer, Karen Phillips, and to tell her what I had done. I really expected Karen to lock me up on the spot, but she was very supportive and told me to take care of it. After more discussion and a few telephone calls, I made an appointment with an investigator from the Harris County District Attorney's office to turn myself in; two days later. I wanted to pick-up all the checks I had written before going in. Sam had agreed to loan me the money to cover all the checks.

Arrangements were made to collect all the checks except one. The check for the airline tickets had been turned in for collection. The investigator was aware of this and had an arrest warrant waiting for me. Since I had two prior convictions in Harris County and was currently on parole, I was held without bond as a habitual criminal.

One week after my arrest, Sam had left on a three week trip for Europe that had been planned for months. I never felt so alone in all my life. I had been in jail for over a week before I even called my parents. I was considering suicide for the second time in as many weeks. The Lord used one of Samantha's employees to reach out to me at this point. I had called Susan to ask her if she would give her a message upon her return. I said, "Tell her I really do love her, but I can't go on." I had decided to go through with the suicide. Susan prayed for me over the phone and I felt a peace come over me I had never known possible.

During the time Sam was gone, she and Doug contacted the owner of the check I had forged and obtained an affidavit stating he did not want to prosecute me. The money had been paid back and he was satisfied. The D.A.'s office decided to press the charges anyway. Two months after my arrest, the judge set a bond in the amount of $75,000 for me. There was no way to obtain that amount of money, so I stayed in jail. Two months after that, he lowered the bond to $10,000 and I was released that night.

In Texas, if indicted and convicted as a habitual criminal, by law, your sentence is to range from 25 to 99 years or life in prison. I knew this when I turned myself in because the thought of leaving the country had crossed my mind. The state offered me twenty-five years as a plea bargain the day I got out on bond, if I would take it then and not go to trial. I could see no bargain in this; not after turning myself in, confessing on tape, and paying back the money.

Since we had the affidavit saying he did not want me prosecuted and the fact that he now lived in California, I felt the chances of him coming back to Houston for a trial were slim. I held out thinking they would dismiss the charges after a year or so. I was wrong once more.

After four months in jail and nine months on bond, we were finally going to trial. In the thirteen months after I had confessed, I had made over forty-two scheduled court appearances. Mary Hennessy, my attorney, and I came to court on Monday morning for a scheduled hearing date. Mary told me we were on "hold-over" until Friday when we would get a reset. This had happen many times before. She even informed me she was about to go on vacation and the next date might not be for another two and a half months (a normal reset was for six weeks). This all changed overnight.

Mary called me at work the next day and said the judge wanted us in court at 1 pm to select a jury; we were scheduled for trial. After selecting a jury, we were told we would start the trial at 10 am the following day. With the exception of the check owner, who was flying in the next day, we were finished with testimony that afternoon. He had flown to New Orleans on business and had agreed to stop back by Houston on his return trip. I really feel the only reason he did was to get the D.A.'s office to stop calling him at home and work. They had been doing this several times a month for the past year. I had waited for 13 months to go to trial and it was now over...in 13 hours of court time.

**GUILTY AS CHARGED**

We stood as the jury came in. After all were seated, Judge Mike McSpadden asked, "Mr. Foreman, has the jury reached a verdict?" 'Yes, your honor.' "What say ye?" 'We the jury, of the 209th District Court of Houston, Harris County, Texas, hereby find the defendant guilty as charged of the offense of forgery and sentence him to forty years in the Texas Department of Corrections."

Mary immediately responded, "Your Honor, we would like the jury polled." We wanted to hear each juror say, "Yes, forty years is my desire for this man." Mary and I both knew I was not being sentenced for this crime, but for the four before this one. People guilty of more serious crimes rarely receive forty years in Texas, All twelve answered in the affirmative. I was now #632374 in the Texas Department of Corrections. I was fortunate I did not get a longer sentence; I deserved one!

(*)Some names have been changed at the request of individuals involved.

# Chapter 9

# *SATAN'S HOLD*

● ● ● ● ● ● ● ● ● ● ● ● ● ● ● ● ● ● ● ● ●

*"Trust in the Lord with all thine heart; and lean not unto thine own understanding. In all thy ways acknowledge Him, and He shall direct thy paths."*

Proverbs 3:5,6

I have used a lot of my Marine Corps training in life to get jobs. I have failed, however, to use the most important thing they taught me. That is, to think everything through, completely, before acting. To look at every possible angle, good and bad, of a problem, then work on a solution. To **act** on a situation, **not-react** to it. If this had been done, I would never have been in jail. If the teachings given me in the early years at church and home had been followed, I would not have been here. At least living in close housing quarters in the military helped me to survive in prison and, with the few exceptions already mentioned, allowed me to get along well with others. Having spent close to five years behind bars before my last conviction, I had been in another prison for over twenty years.

A prison, I, with the help of Satan and his deception, began building years before. After hearing for so long, "Why can't you be more like your brothers", from others and later from myself, I had come to believe that I could not be accepted as myself. The need to prove myself to others, to be liked and accepted, had caused me to enter into a silent competition against my brothers. I felt the need to prove I was as good as they were; that I could have the things they had, all to make me "look good" in the eyes of others. The need to feel important and wanted was very critical to me. All of this was in my mind, not the minds of others. I only thought that was what they were thinking. Satan had lied to and deceived me for so long, I believed it. When you really believe something, it becomes truth; it becomes real to you.

It must be said here, in no way do I want to take away from my brother's success. They have worked very hard and long hours to get where they are in life. I tried the easy route, without the work, and it <u>did not</u> work!! Not once did they contribute to the feelings I had. They have always been very loving toward me. This was <u>all</u> Satan and me. I love my brothers very much and always have.

Today, psychologist call this problem, low self-esteem or low self-image. True, part of it was that. This is one cause of low self-esteem; when others tell you that you are not "acceptable" as you are, that you should be like someone else, and you believe them. "A low self-esteem is a threat to the entire human family and affects all levels of society, all races and cultures, according to Dr. James Dobson of **Focus on the Family**.[1] As I know realize, Satan is the king of lies and deception and mine was more of a problem with him. He will do anything he can to get into your life and destroy it, if **YOU** allow him to. His primary weapon against you is deception. He will lie to you to the point you will lie to yourself and then to others. He will hit you twice as hard if he sees you are a follower of Jesus Christ and trying to live your life for Christ. That is the last thing Satan wants.

The time when my "prison walls" were going up, I had felt the call into full-time ministry, to preach the Gospel. The problem was, Christ was never made the Lord over my life. Satan attacked me head-on. When I left home to enter the military, I, like so many others, slipped from my Christian walk. I tended to forget Christ in the good times, only thinking of Him in times of need. Now, I know that He is **ALWAYS** needed. But it was too late; Satan was already at work.

I have had people tell me, "Alan, what you have done is not that bad. You did not kill, hurt or rape anyone. You did not attack some small child and you have never been a drug addict or alcoholic." **So what?!** Are those the only crimes or wrongs that we look at in life? It does not matter!! What I did was a crime and it was wrong, regardless of what "degree" you put on it. That is one problem we have today in our society; we put "degrees" on right and wrong to fit our own needs. We have taken prayer out of public school classrooms. Prayer and Bible study have been taken out of some churches. There are people rewriting the Bible changing God's gender and His reference to the sexes to fit their current view on life! Do you know that right now, there is more of a revival in some prisons than there is in the "free-world" church. Praise God for it! Men in prisons are more at peace and are freer behind bars than a lot of people walking the streets.

The reason why I gave into temptation to forge that first check is still a mystery to me. It would have been so easy to just return the check with an explanation. Perhaps it was the thrill of risk. I have lived my life on the edge most of the time. I do know the last four convictions came about for the same reason.

I was role playing; trying to be someone I was not. Trying to impress others with who I was or with what I had to be liked and accepted. Accepted, not for who I was, but who **I thought** others wanted me to be. My identity was in the wrong place. I had been living my life for over twenty years to please everyone except the One I should have...Jesus Christ.

I had often set my goals and dreams at levels that could not possibly be reached. When I failed to achieve them, matters became worse than before. I have always wanted everything right now; no work, no wait, just let it be. Please do not take this the wrong way. Everyone needs to have their goals in life. Just be realistic when you set them for yourself.

My role playing and living in a fantasy world caused me to lie to others. One lie led to another, and another to cover up the first. It never ended. Not only was I a habitual criminal, I was also a habitual and compulsive liar. My whole life had been a lie to others and myself. Lies that destroyed my marriage, friendships, jobs, and led to prison time...real prison time.

By the grace of God, I have finally realized that my problems have been caused by two primary things:

1) My desire to impress others with how important I was and;

2) My desire for material success becoming greater than my interest in the welfare of my fellow man.

I have now learned more of that foundation stone of character, which is honesty. I have learned that when we act upon the highest conception of honesty which is given to us, our sense of honesty becomes more acute. I have learned that honesty is truth, and according to John 8:32,

**"...the truth will set you free..."**

How true it is! I am still facing many years[2] in prison as I write this, but I have a peace in my soul that far surpasses the fact I am still behind bars. The prison Satan created for me has been destroyed...completely and forever.

---

[1] Dobson, James. <u>What Wives Wish Their Husbands Knew About Women</u>. Wheaton, Tyndale, 1975 (p 24).
[2] Alan's projected release date from Texas Department of Corrections is February 2008.

# Chapter 10

# *CHRIST IS THE ANSWER*

• • • • • • • • • • • • • • • • • • • •

*"Jesus said to him, 'I am the Way and the Truth and the Life; no man cometh unto the Father, but by me."*

*John 14:6*

Even though this nation is on the decline today, we still have a wonderful environment; yet our people are not happy. They are not satisfied. Suicides, drug addiction, alcoholism, child abuse and homosexuality are at all time highs. The more material prosperity people gain, the less happiness they seem to have. The standard of living is higher here than in any other part of the globe, yet there is little real happiness, for happiness does not come from the things we possess. It took me a long time to realize this. Happiness also does not come from our association. It does not come from the stimulation of praise or approbation. It only comes in one way, a personal relationship with God through Jesus Christ, His Son, and by claiming, in faith, the grace provisions that He has for us after salvation.

We need to learn to be occupied with Jesus Christ! The believer who is not occupied with Christ is a very lonely and miserable person, no matter who he is or what he has. If you are a believer in Christ and you have your eyes on yourself, you are set up for misery. A close companion of "eyes-on-self" is "eyes-on-others." These two usually coordinate and run together. If you have your eyes on yourself, you also have a tendency to get your eyes on others, for you interpret people in the light of your sensitivity. Too many believers are ultra-sensitive to what other people think and consequently are totally miserable.

You will never have strength, power or blessing until you come to the place of occupation with Christ - until He is truly the One who holds first place in your life. The moment you get eyes on self and begin to feel sorry for yourself or to magnify yourself, the instant you get eyes on others and get upset whenever they cross you, whenever you start looking at material things, then you have become open and vulnerable to satanic attack. Our biggest battle right now is not the famine in Africa, it is not the uprising in Bosnia, it is not the homeless in America, and it is not the economy or unemployment problems. Our biggest battle right now is a spiritual warfare of powers and principalities we can not even see and Satan is the commanding general.

> **"For we are not wrestling with flesh and blood but against the despotisms, against the powers, against rulers of this present darkness, against the spirit forces of wickedness in the heavenly sphere."**
> **Ephesians 6:12 (AMP.)**

You have got to get occupied with Christ, first by gaining knowledge of Him through His Word, the Bible. You have to know Him to be occupied with Him. Second, you must be filled with the Holy Spirit. Without these, you can not be occupied with Christ. Occupation with Christ is absolutely vital and necessary if you are to have true happiness or peace as a Christian. Salvation alone will not give you this happiness.

Once you become a Christian and have your salvation, the standard of happiness is based - not upon any human factor in life, but upon your occupation with Christ and the resultant pre-eminence of the Lord in your Life. Since, along with salvation, it is a part of the Father's plan that Christ should always have first place, this is the **only** way a believer can have true happiness.

> **"And He is the head of the body, the church, who is the beginning, the firstborn from the dead, that in all things He may have the preeminence."**
> **Colossians 1:18 (NKJV)**

Can you look back over the past week and say, "In every set of circumstances, Christ has been in first place?" If not, you need the in-filling of the Spirit, followed by occupation with Christ. This in-filling of the Spirit is a daily process. Colossians 3:10 shows us this.

> **"And have clothed yourselves with the new [spiritual self], which is [ever in the process of being] re-newed and remolded into [fuller and more perfect knowledge upon] knowledge after the image (the likeness) of Him Who create it." (AMP.)**

Only then can He be preeminent; only then can He be glorified. Christ can not be glorified before the unbeliever until He is glorified in your life.

> **"clearly you are an epistle of Christ, ministered by us, written not with ink but by the Spirit of the living God, not on tablets of stone but on tablets of flesh, that is, of the heart."**
> **2 Corinthians 3:3 (NKJV)**

Another problem so many of us have, or had, is when things do not go our way, we try to change everyone or everything...except ourselves. Since, **"...Christ is the same yesterday, today and forever"** (Heb 13:8), then there is only one person we need to think about changing; Ourselves. When you can master this, you have just fixed a major problem. No matter how exasperating someone may be, you can not change them. There is only one person in the world you can change and it is you! Husbands, you can not change your wives. Teenagers, you can not change your boyfriend or girlfriends. Parents, you can not change your children. You can only change you! As long as you keep trying to change others, you are going to generate strife, hard feelings and pain with them and yourself.

Finally, you must forget the past. Failure in this area is probably responsible for more problems than any other single factor in our lives.

GUILTY AS CHARGED

> **"Brethren, I count myself not to have appre-**
> **hended: but this one thing I do, forgetting**
> **those things which are behind, and reaching**
> **forth unto those things which are before, I**
> **press toward the mark for the prize of the high**
> **calling of God in Jesus Christ."**
> **Philippians 3:13-14**

Paul tells us here, we need to forget the past so we can reach the great things of the future. These verses apply to **every** area of a believer's life. Focusing on the past will only weigh you down and prevent you from seeing the future promises of God.

What do you need to forget? Just two types of things: the good and the bad. That's right. The good as well as the bad. Here is why. If you dwell on the good in your past, you will soon become dissatisfied in yourself and become resentful of the way things are now. You will also allow Satan in your life with grief and despair. It will also distort your perception of the present and your hope for the future. The only part of your past you need to remember are the victories you have in Jesus Christ. **NO MORE!** If you only remember the victories in the past, it will increase your confidence, self-image and faith.

Now for the bad. If you need to forget the good, you <u>know</u> you need to rid the bad as well. As tough as it may be, you have to let go. If you do not, these bad memories will produce the fruit of unforgiveness - toward yourself, others and God. In order to forgive, you <u>**must**</u> forget. Even God will forget it. If He can, why shouldn't you?

> **"I, even I, am he that blotteth out thy trans-**
> **gressions for mine own sake, and will not**
> **remember thy sins."**
> **Isaiah 43:25**

Jesus also said in Luke 9:62, **"No one, having put his hand to the plow, and looking back, is fit for the kingdom of God."** So you can see, we really do need to forget.

You need to do two things to forget those painful memories. Our first clue comes from Paul in Philippians 4:8. He says,

> **"Finally, brethren, whatsoever things are true, whatsoever things are honest, whatsoever things are just, whatsoever things are pure, whatsoever things are lovely; whatsoever things are of good report; if there be any virtue, and if there be any praise, think on these thing."**

You might say now, "Alan, what satisfies or covers these requirements?" To me, only Jesus Christ's death on the cross and His resurrection. Was it true - Yes. Was it just in the eyes of God - Yes. Was it pure - Very much so. Was it lovely - Yes. Was it gracious - Yes. Was it worthy of praise - Yes. All of these answers are yes, a thousand times over!

Rest assured, Satan will remind you of every rotten, no good, insensitive thing you have ever done. But when this happens, **YOU** must redirect your thoughts to the good.

The second thing you need to do is stop basing your actions on the past. James 1:22-25 tells us if we want the Word of God to work for us, we must do more than just hear it, we have to act on it.

> **"But be ye doers of the word, and not hearers only deceiving your own selves..."**

That works in the negative as well. If you want to stop dwelling in the past, you must start acting like it never happen! Stop beating yourself down with your past actions. God has forgiven you and blotted it out, no longer to remember them. You should, too. The **only** thing keeping you from forgetting is **you**!!

Jesus Christ has already defeated these powers and principalities and has given us the victory, according to Colossians 2:15.

> **"...having spoiled principalities and powers, He made a show of them openly, triumphing over them in it."**

Why not let Him do it for you?

GUILTY AS CHARGED

**GUILTY AS CHARGED**

# Chapter 11

# *ANGELS IN DISGUISE*

● ● ● ● ● ● ● ● ● ● ● ● ● ● ● ● ● ● ● ● ● ●

*"I know that whatever God does, it shall be forever.
Nothing can be added to it, and nothing taken from it.
God does it, that men should fear before Him."*

*Ecclesiastes 3:14*

Regardless of where I have lived, the Lord has always had one or two people in each location to watch over me who have had a large impact on me in establishing my Christian foundation. Some of these people I have known a very long time. Others were just in passing, where names, if ever I knew them, now escape me. All of them have been my "angels in disguise." Several were mentioned throughout the book. Others, I would like to introduce to you now.

As a teenager growing up, my pastor at the First Baptist Church in Homer, Dr. Billy K. Smith, and minister of music/youth, W.A. "Sonny" Steed, played an ever important role in setting a solid foundation for me. At the same time, "The Prophets", David Talley and Charles Gloer, influenced me greatly with their ministry in music and song. I was fortunate to travel with these two young men as a sound technician while in high school and I have carried their music with me for years. **Thank you**, all four, for the valuable lessons you taught.

In Moscow, career diplomat, Ambassador Walter J. Stoessal was like a second father to me. This man's moral and ethical standards were second to none. My memory of him will carry on for years to come.

Doug & Sarita Cox will always have a special place in my heart for taking me into their "family" in Hot Springs. The

Christian influence they had on me will always be remembered and cherished.

More recently, the people who displayed more love and understanding than I knew possible. A big Thank You goes out to the members of the Singles Department of Kingsland Baptist Church during 1990-92, led by Director Jeanette Moody and Teacher Doug Rimmer. These people were used by the Lord to show me, for the first time in my life, that I could be accepted for who I was. Some shared of their own previous problems and/or those of family members. They provided much needed support by way of prayers, visits, cards and letters, and friendship to myself and family. Because of the love they shared, I dropped the name taken upon leaving the federal prison and took back my birth name. I realized that I had to be me, not someone made up.

There are not words enough to thank Pam Whitcomb for her service to the Lord in song. He has given her a beautiful voice which she uses to praise Him and to touch the hearts of all that hear her. Pam's singing of **"He's Been Faithful"** first started me looking inside myself. When first hearing this song, it was felt Pam knew my entire life story and had put it to music. Thank you, Pam, for showing me that He is faithful...always.

With all the time spent behind bars, I thought I was the only one being hurt. Restitution had been made to my victims and I never physically hurt anyone with my crimes. I was the only one in jail, so I thought I was the only one hurt. It was never considered how my actions were tearing my family and friends apart. Not until a letter was received from a friend after my last conviction. It came from a then, seventeen year old girl who was a friend and a daughter of a class member at Kingsland. Her name: Carrie Fennell. This young lady showed in a two page letter, what I had failed, and refused, to see in twenty years. It showed how a sweet, innocent girl, whom I never intended to hurt, was almost destroyed by my deception and lies to her and her mother. She showed me that my actions affect <u>everyone</u> around me, not just myself. Carrie's letter was a major turning point in my life and the inspiration for this book. I love you, Carrie!

Thank you, Susan Stokes, for allowing the Lord to use you; for listening to His call and going forth, in faith, with your actions. Thank you for being the child of God that you are.

**GUILTY AS CHARGED**

Where would I be right now if not for **Samantha\***? Without the love and support of this lady, in ways too many to mention, I might not be here today. This wonderful lady was lied to, deceived, robbed, was investigated by the D.A.'s office and yet, displayed an unconditional love for the person that did all this to her...me. The Lord used Sam in my life when nothing else that I know of would have reached me. She has been beside me 110% through everyday of this last ordeal. Sam is the best friend I have and has become the sister I never had.

My family...two of the most wonderful and loving parents God ever placed in anyone's life and two very special brothers. Thank you all, for standing beside me, no matter what I have done or how many times I did it. You had every right to kick me out, long ago, with instructions never to return. I praise God you did not. I can not say, "I'm sorry" enough to cover all that has been done to you. "I'm sorry" even becomes empty and void of meaning, if used that many times. I can only promise, from this point forward, I will live my life in such a manner that "I'm sorry" will not be needed again.

A special thank you to Dr. James Dobson and the "Focus on the Family" organization for their dedication to the ministry of the Lord. Their support and resources make such an impact on many, many people, both in and out of prison.

Though listed last, in order of importance should be first, I thank my savior, Jesus Christ. For without Him, I would not be at the point in my life now to ask forgiveness of all of you. To even confront you with the truth is a miracle of God. It hurt so much to be honest with myself after so long; it hurt even more so to admit it to you. But through the pain, I am reminded of a scripture we all need to remember:

> **"For I reckon that the sufferings of this present time are not worthy to be compared with the glory which shall be revealed in us."**
> **Romans 8:18**

Before, I did not know what real love was. Through Him, I have learned to love, truly love, others. I am learning to turn negative thoughts and emotions over to the Lord, and am allowing the forgiving love of Christ to replace them. Most important, I have been able to forgive myself and begin the process of accepting myself.

I do not doubt that God is a loving Father and He never **causes** harm to come to any of His children. He does make good use of the trouble **we** bring on ourselves to teach us; to help us grow spiritually. There have been no less than six times in my life, where because of what I was doing, I should be dead now. God did not keep me from death six times, or more, for no reason! He has a plan and purpose for my life and He now has my attention to teach me what He wants me to know. I no longer blame others for my problems. I take full responsibility for my actions. Before, I would only do so if confronted.

Jesus loves all of us very much. I had heard and read John 3:16 all of my life, but until Dan Gilbert explained it in a different way from before, I never saw just how much He did love me. Dan told me to insert my name into the verse every time it was read to make it personal. Boy did that open my eyes! Let me show you:

**"For God so loved Alan, that He gave His only begotten Son, that should Alan believe in Him, Alan will not die, but Alan will have eternal life."**
**John 3:16**

Isn't that wonderful! Thank you, Dan, for sharing that with me and now with others. God loves you the same way. Do you dare give Jesus a chance in your life? I pray you will.

Where are you going with your life? Are you accepting responsibility for your actions? Do you love, really love, others as Jesus does? If not and you have no real happiness in your life, no joy and peace within your soul, perhaps you will give Jesus a try. If alcohol and drugs did not help, Jesus can. If money and material possessions did not give you what you expected, believe me, Jesus will.

I heard a song a few years back that ended something like this: "We are the champions, my friends. And we'll keep on fighting till the end. We are the champions, we are the champions, we are the champions of the world..." As a follower of Christ, a believer and doer of His Word, you can be a champion. But, like the song says, you will have to fight till the end. Then, and only then, will we be the champions of the world. The good thing is, Christ will be there with you every step of the way; you are not by yourself. He wants to help you, He can help you, He will help you, but He will not force you. It is your decision-what will it be?

Do you feel like a nobody or a somebody? Are you a loser or a winner? Are you a chump or a champ? If you want to be a champ, there is only one way; through Jesus Christ. If you are wiling to join in the battle of all times, in a fight to the end, Jesus Christ welcomes you with open arms and He will make you a champion.

> **"But thanks be to God, Who gives us the victory through our Lord Jesus Christ."**
> **1 Corinthians 15:57**

(*) Some names have been changed at the request of individuals involved.

# PART 2

## YOUR TRUE IDENTITY:
### You Are Somebody!!

# Chapter 12

# *YOU ARE SOMEBODY!!*

● ● ● ● ● ● ● ● ● ● ● ● ● ● ● ● ● ● ●

*Your greatest glory is not in never falling, but in
rising each time you fall.*

In Part 1, you were told of the many jobs held and the problems encountered in my life. It showed you that I had made the mistake so many others have made in placing my identity in what I did or in what I had. To me, this was success; having material possessions and having an "important" job to impress others. I felt that being accepted by others would give me the happiness I longed for. I was wrong!!

Having heard most of my teenage life that I was not good enough the way I was and hearing "Why can't you be more like your brothers", I had accepted my identity as one who was not good enough and, through time, acquired what was believed to be low self-esteem or low self-image. Dr. Dobson states that, "...at least 90 percent of our self-concept is built from what **WE** think others think about us..."[1] I have come to learn that it was, to an extent, low self-image, but it was more of an improper self-image.

It was not until I found and placed my identity, my true identity, in Jesus Christ as my Lord and Savior that true happiness came to me. It is my prayer and desire that in this short time we share together, that you will be able to see your true identity as well; who you **really are** in Jesus Christ so that you, too, may have this happiness that I have found.

The Bible is divided into two parts; The Old and New Testaments with thirty-nine books in the Old Testament and twenty-seven books in the New Testament. In the New Testament, we have the four Gospels, telling of Christ's life on earth: the Book of Acts, a book of history; twenty-one books called the Epistles, which were written to the church, we as Christians; and one book of prophecy, Revelation. In the Epistles, I have found some 130 verses that contain the words **In Christ, In Him,** or **In Whom.** It was not until I began reading and studying these verses that I began to see my true identity. You see, in these verses, it tells us who we are in Christ Jesus and what we have, as promises, In Him. This is where we learn our true identity.

This is where we will be looking in the next few chapters. We will not cover all of these verses, but we will cover some very important ones to help you see who you are and where your true identity lies.

The importance of personal identity can not be exaggerated. But immeasurably more important is our spiritual identity. Do we know whether we are an accidental product of a mindless process of evolution or whether we are God's creation made in His image? Before we begin looking at the Epistles, let's go to Genesis and look at our beginning on earth.

> **"Then God said, 'Let Us make man in Our image, according to Our likeness; let them have dominion over the fish of the sea, over the birds of the air, and over the cattle, over all the earth and every creeping thing that creeps on the earth." So God created man in His image; in the image of God He created him; male and female He created them.'"**
> **Genesis 1:26-27 NKJV**

As you can see, God made us in His own image and that is our first point to remember. The Book of Genesis goes on to tell us how God placed man in the Garden of Eden to work it and to take care of it (Genesis 2:15-17). God told man that he could eat from any tree in the garden except the tree of knowledge of good and evil. If man were to eat of this tree, he would die. Genesis 3:1-13 goes on to tell us how man made his decision to eat of the forbidden fruit. At this point, man fell from his appointed place God had given him and from God's plan for us. This is further described to us in the book of Romans. Paul tells us in Romans 5:12:

> **"Therefore, just as through one man sin entered the world, and death through sin, and thus death spread to all men, because all sinned –" NKJV**

Through Adam's decision to eat of the fruit, he brought sin into the world and thus brought death, spiritual and physical death, upon all of us. This is again shown in Romans 3:23:

> **"for all have sinned and come short of the glory of God."**

Paul goes on to show us the payment for this sin in Romans 6:23:

> **"For the wages of sin is death, but the gift of God is eternal life IN JESUS CHRIST our Lord." NKJV**

Through Adam, we have all sinned and since the wages of sin is death, we are all spiritually dead. But one of our promises **In Christ** is that we have eternal life.

Well, you say now, "Alan, why would I want to have eternal life when life now doesn't seem worth living?" That is where the promises of God that we have **In Christ** come into play. What good is a promise or a gift if you do not know that you have it? It is like the old story of the man who had a thousand dollars deposited into his checking account, but he knew nothing about it. The money was very much his, but what good did it do him if he knew nothing of it? You have to know what the promises of God are to you to benefit from them.

I once heard Bob George give an example that I feel explains what I am speaking of very well.[2] Bob told a story of a king that had decided to pardon all the prostitutes in his kingdom for their crimes. Did this pardon give the prostitutes any incentive to change their life styles? Not really. On the other hand, what if the king was attracted to one of the women and decided to marry her. Knowing that her life, as a queen, would now be much better than before, she would have no interest in returning to her old ways would she? Of course not! We as Christians are the same way. Even though our heavenly Father has pardoned us from our sins by giving His only Son for us, we need to know what we have **In Him** and what He has for us before we can realize that our previous life is not worth hanging on to. Once we know what we have **In Him** or **In Christ** then our life changes. Once we realize that Christ is not just a man that lived and died some 2000 years ago, but that He is the Living God of today, who is living within us, walking with us every step we make, then and only then does this life that does not seem worth living become a new and exciting life that you can not do without.

Go with me now as we look at some of the promises we have **In Christ**.

---

[1] Dobson, James. <u>What Wives Wish...</u> (p 24)
[2] Bob George is founder and president of Discipleship Counseling Services of Dallas, Texas, and the counselor and teacher on the **"People to People"** radio program.

**Chapter 13**

# *THE CHOSEN ONES*

● ● ● ● ● ● ● ● ● ● ● ● ● ● ● ● ● ● ● ●

*"Blessed is the nation whose God is the Lord; and the people
whom He hath chosen for His own inheritance."*
*Psalms 33:12*


We have listed a few of the promises we have **In Him** in the
previous chapter. Let us now look at each of these and the
Scripture that support these issues.

Our first is CHOSEN. The word chosen, in the following verses, comes from the Greek word eklego, meaning, "to pick out;
select" according to Vines.[1]  Three verses that tell us of God's
choice of us are shown to us in the following verses written by
Paul. In Ephesians 1:4, Paul tells us:

> **"just as He chose us IN HIM before the foun-
> dation of the world, that we should be holy
> and without blame before Him in love." (NKJV)**

2 Thessalonians 2:13 reinforces the previous verse in letting us
know how God felt about us **before** the world was formed.

> **"But we are bound to give thanks to God
> always for you, brethren beloved by the Lord,
> because God from the beginning chose you
> for salvation through sanctification by the
> Spirit and belief in the truth" (NKJV)**

One other verse that I have found that not only confirms that we
are chosen, but also that it is a promise of God is James 2:5.

> **"Hearken, my beloved brethren, did not God choose the poor of the world to be rich in faith, and heirs of the kingdom which He promised to those who love Him?" (ASW)**

1 Peter 2:9 tells us that we are not only chosen, but are His special people. This verse has been a comfort to me when feeling rejected. Let's look at it together.

> **"But you are a CHOSEN generation, a royal priesthood, a holy nation, His own special people, that you may proclaim the praises of Him who called you out of darkness into His marvelous light" (NKJV)**

Isn't it great to know that He wants us, that He has already chosen us for His own!! Just the fact of knowing that should give you the hope you need to continue on in life and to look deeper into His Word for other promises.

---

[1] Vine, W.E. Vine's Complete Expository Dictionary of Old and New Testament Words. Nashville, Thomas Nelson, 1985 (pp100-101).

# Chapter 14

# *THE FORGIVEN*

• • • • • • • • • • • • • • • • • • • •

*To understand the Trinity is to lose one's mind;*
*But to deny the Trinity is to lose one's soul.*

Forgiven, 1. to cease to blame or feel resentment about (an offense or offender). 2. to cancel or let off (a debt). 3. to bestow a favor unconditionally.[1]

This is what God has done for all of us through His Son Jesus Christ. Many of us have done things in our lives that were wrong, things that we are now ashamed of. Maybe we have been caught and punished by the law or maybe it went unnoticed and we got away. Even if we got away from the law, God saw us do everything that we have ever done. Isn't it nice to know that He has pardoned us from these wrongs so that they will not be held over us the rest of our lives? You bet it is!! You say, "Alan, how do you know He has forgiven me. How do you know that we have been pardoned from these offenses?" Because He says so in His Word. All we have to do is confess our sins to Him and accept His forgiveness that He has already provided through the death of His Son Jesus. Look at 1 John 1:9 with me.

> **"If we confess our sins, He is faithful and just**
> **to forgive us our sins and to cleanse us from**
> **all unrighteousness."**

John goes on in 1 John 2:12 to explain that these sins are forgiven because of His Son.

> **"I write to you, little children, Because your**
> **sins <u>are forgiven</u> you for His name's sake."**

GUILTY AS CHARGED

In Colossians 2:13, Paul reaffirms John's message to us.

> **"And you, being dead in your trespasses and the uncircumcision of your flesh, He has made alive together with Him, having forgiven you all trespasses."**

The Amplified version is one that I really like for this verse.

> **"And you were dead in trespasses and in the uncircumcision of your flesh (your sensuality, your sinful carnal nature), [God] brought life together with [Christ], having [freely] forgiven us all our transgressions"** **(AMP.)**

Even though we were still living according to the flesh, God still forgave us of our sins. But, we must remember, if God is to forgive us our sins, we must forgive others of their sins against us. Paul makes this very clear to us in Ephesians 4:32.

> **"And be kind to one another, tenderhearted, forgiving one another, even as God <u>IN CHRIST</u> forgave you." (NKJV)**

This is a very important part of receiving forgiveness from the Lord. We **must** forgive others as God forgave us.

---

[1] Vine's, (pp 250-251)

**Chapter 15**

# *A NEW CREATION*

● ● ● ● ● ● ● ● ● ● ● ● ● ● ● ● ● ● ●

*Whatever lies behind you and whatever lies before you is
of no comparison to what lies within you.*

Even though we have lived in sin, through Jesus Christ, we
have been reconciled to God and can be placed back into His
plan for us. All we have to do is to accept the grace provision He
has given as a free gift to all. Once we accept Christ as our Lord
and Savior, all of our sins are forgiven and we become new
creatures. As 2 Corinthians 5:17 tells us, being IN CHRIST
makes us new.

> **"Therefore, if anyone is IN CHRIST he is a new
> creation: old things have passed away:
> behold, all things have become new." (NKJV)**

This is one of our promises and part of our true identity. In Christ,
we are a new creation.

We are a new creation, but what does that mean. You look in
the mirror and see the same old self and say, "I'm no different
than I was before." Remember how we talked about being made
in the image of God. Well, God is a spirit (John 4:24). If God is a
spirit, then man is a spirit. After all, man was created in the image
of God. In fact, man is a spirit, he has a soul and he lives in a
body. When the Lord said you were a new creation, He was talk-
ing about your inner being or your spirit. Let us look at
Colossians 3:10 to yet a better understanding of this.

> **"and have put on the new man who is renewed
> in knowledge according to the image of Him
> who created him," (NKJV)**

Once again, let us look in the Amplified for further reference of this same verse.

> **"And have clothed yourselves with the new [spiritual self], which is [ever in the process of being] renewed and remolded into [fuller and more perfect knowledge upon] knowledge after the image (the likeness) of Him Who created it." (Amp.)**

Ephesians 4:24 is another verse that shows us this as well.

> **"and put on the new man, who after God was created in righteousness and holiness of the truth." (ASW)**

What does it mean to put on the new man? It means to put on Christ, by putting on more and more of His holy nature - especially His love, kindness, humility, etc. We have to study His Word to know Him and to see how He wants us to be; in His likeness.

# Chapter 16

# *A TEMPLE OF GOD*

● ● ● ● ● ● ● ● ● ● ● ● ● ● ● ● ● ● ● ● ●

*Let go & let God!*

For the longest time, I only thought of Christ as a human that lived upon the earth some 2000 years ago. A man that performed miracles while here and then was crucified on a cross for His way of life. I saw Him as a man that died on the cross and was buried in a tomb. I tend to feel that many Christians today do the same thing. They only see Him as the wonderful Son of God that gave His life so that they may have eternal life **AFTER** they die and leave earth.

What we have to remember is that He did die on the cross, but He arose from the dead and He is the living God who gives us our life today. Without Him, we have no life. HE IS ALIVE!!!! It is as plain as can be if we will only believe the Word of God. In 2 Corinthians 6:16, Paul shows this without any doubts.

> **"....For you are the temple of the living God. As God has said: "I will dwell in them and walk among them. I will be their God and they shall be My people.'" (NKJV)**

If then, He is the living God and He is dwelling within us, then our bodies are the home or temple of God. God is living inside of us. We are His home. 1 Corinthians 6:19-20 shows us this.

> **"Or do you not know that your body is the temple of the Holy Spirit who is in you, whom you have from God and you are not your own?**

**For you were bought at a price; therefore glorify God in your body and in your spirit, which are God's." (NKJV)**

The body of every truly converted person belongs to the Holy Spirit to use as His temple. What a crime it must be to pollute the body, to rob Him of His rightful abode! What unspeakable wrong is such a course upon the believer himself.

# Chapter 17

# *ALIVE FOR EVERMORE*

● ● ● ● ● ● ● ● ● ● ● ● ● ● ● ● ● ● ● ●

*"...It cannot be emphasized too strongly or too often that this great nation was founded NOT by religionists BUT by Christians, NOT on religions BUT on the Gospel of Jesus Christ."*
*- Patrick Henry*

Each one of us has life in our bodies. Otherwise we would not be able to walk, talk, and do the things we do. But is having life and being alive the same thing? What does it really mean to be alive? I have come to realize that being alive is not worrying...about my next meal, what I will wear, or what type of work I may be doing. Being alive is having joy and peace in your life. Not happy one minute and down in deep depression the next. Being alive means knowing that Christ is right there with you every step of the way through every trial that comes your way. Christ is in you: Christ is your life. You can not possibly live the Christian life on your own. You just can not do it. It is impossible!! The only way to live the Christian life is to let Christ live through you. Let others see Christ in you, not you trying to live like Christ. The only way to be alive is through Jesus Christ. Romans 6:9-11 will start us off to see this.

> **"knowing that Christ, having been raised from the dead, dies no more. Death no longer has dominion over Him. For the death that He died, He died to sin once for all; but the life that He lives, He lives to God. Likewise you also, reckon yourselves to be dead to sin, but alive to God IN CHRIST JESUS our Lord. (NKJV)**

We spoke earlier how through Adam we were all made dead, spiritually, but through Christ, we can be made alive. Let's look at three more verses that help us to see this more clearly.

> **"For as Adam all die, even so IN CHRIST all shall be made alive."**
> **1 Corinthians 15:22   (NKJV)**

> **"even when we were dead in trespasses, made us alive together WITH CHRIST (by grace you have been saved), and raised us up together, and made us sit together in the heavenly places IN CHRIST JESUS."**
> **Ephesians 2:5-6 (NKJV)**

> **"For Christ also suffered once for sins, the just for the unjust, that He might bring us to God, being put to death in the flesh but made alive by the spirit."**
> **1 Peter 3:18 (NKJV)**

> **"For Christ [the Messiah Himself] died for sins once for all, the Righteous for the unrighteous (the just for the unjust, the innocent for the guilty), that He might bring us to God. In His human body He was put to death, but He was made alive in the spirit."**
> **1 Peter 3:18 (AMP.)**

These verses make it very plain to see, Christ is the **only** way for us to be made alive. We can not do anything on our own to obtain this except for receiving Jesus Christ into our lives as our Lord and Savior.

# Chapter 18

# *CHILD OF GOD &*
# *JOINT HEIRS*

• • • • • • • • • • • • • • • • • • • • •

*You were born an original; Do not die a copy!!*

We have now seen that **IN CHRIST**, we are the chosen, the forgiven, new creations, that our bodies are the temple of God, and that we are alive **IN HIM**. That, in itself is so wonderful, but it gets better. Let's look at the next two promises together.

Do you remember the story of the king that married the prostitute? By becoming a queen, she had no desire to return to her past life style. Neither should you, because you are a child of God. That's right!! You are a kid of the Kingdom!! John tells us that we are His children and will be like Him when He returns.

> **"Behold what manner of love the Father hath given to us, that we should be called children of God; and such we are. For this cause the world knows us not, because it knew Him not. Beloved, now are we children of God, and never yet was it manifested what we shall be. Know that, if He shall be manifested, we shall be like Him, because we shall see Him as He is." John 3:1-2 ASW.**

Paul tells us in Romans, that not only are we children of God, but also joint-heirs with Christ. If we are joint-heirs, we are entitled to all the glory Christ has and it is through Christ that this is available.

> **"The Spirit Himself bears witness with our spirit that we are children of God, and if children, then heirs - joint heirs with Christ and heirs of God, if indeed we suffer with Him, that we may also be glorified together."**
> **Romans 8:16-17 NKJV**

Paul assures us in several other verses of our promise to be heirs.

> **"And if ye are Christ's, ye are, consequently, Abraham's seed, and heirs according to promise." Galatians 3:29 ASW.**

"If ye are in Christ"; if you belong to Him and are united to Him by a living faith. The Book of Hebrews tells us, "That without faith, it is impossible to please Him" (Hebrews 11:6). You have to believe in Him and have faith in Him to see and carry you through life by His living within you.

> **"that the Gentiles should be fellow heirs, of the same body, and partakers of His promise IN CHRIST through the gospel,"**
> **Ephesians 3:6**

Isn't it great to know your Father is a king!! The King of all kings and Lord of all lords... You could have no better life than the one He offers to you. But that is all He will do; offer it to you. It is up to you to decide if you want it or not. **YOU** have to decide!

# Chapter 19

# REDEEMED BY
# THE BLOOD

● ● ● ● ● ● ● ● ● ● ● ● ● ● ● ● ● ● ●

*Not a palace, but a stable... Not fine linen, but plain straw...*
*Not nobleman, but shepherds... Not a baby, but our Lord!*

REDEEMED, taken from the Greek word apolutrosis, means "a releasing for (i.e., on payment of) a ransom.¹ Jesus Christ has redeemed us from the justice we deserve. He has paid the ransom for us with His life. there can be no greater price paid by anyone. Paul has given us many Scriptures to show that Christ has done this for us. Let's look at a few of them.

> **"being justified freely by His grace through the redemption that is IN CHRIST JESUS."**
> **Romans 3:24 NKJV**

> **"But of Him, you are IN CHRIST JESUS, who became for us wisdom from God - and right-eousness and sanctification and redemption -"**
> **1 Corinthians 1:30 NKJV**

> **"IN HIM we have redemption through His blood, the forgiveness of sins, according to the riches of His grace"**
> **Ephesians 1:7 NKJV**

> **"IN WHOM we have redemption, the forgive-ness of sins"**
> **Colossians 1:14 ASW.**

Should you read Galatians 3:13, you would see that Christ has redeemed us from the curse of the law by His death on the cross. The curse of the law Paul speaks of is the curse listed in Deuteronomy 28 in the Old Testament. We could write another book altogether on the curse of the law and all that Christ has done for us through the power of His blood. But, perhaps you will take the time to study this on your own. I sure hope so.

---

[1] Vine's, (pp 515-516)

# Chapter 20

# *THE RIGHTEOUSNESS OF GOD*

• • • • • • • • • • • • • • • • • • • •

*Before you turn your back on Jesus, Take a look at His!!*

Do you think, after reading this book, that you are as righteous, in the eyes of God, as I am? Do you feel you are as righteous, in the eyes of God, as say, Charles Stanley or Billy Graham? Do you think you could ever be as righteous, in the eyes of God, as the Apostle Paul who wrote most of the New Testament? Now for the tough part...Do you think God would ever look at you and say, "You are as righteous as my Son, Jesus Christ?" Well, what do you think? If you are anything like I was, you had to say, "NO" to all the above. But before you rule yourself out and say you might as well give up now, let's look at a few verses.

> **"But of Him you are <u>IN CHRIST JESUS</u>, who became for us wisdom from God - and righteousness and sanctification and redemption."**
> **1 Corinthians 1:30 NKJV**

> **"Him Who knew no sin He made to be sin on our behalf, that we may become God's righteousness <u>IN HIM</u>." 2 Corinthians 5:21 ASW**

Worrell goes on to explain in his footnotes that the Father laid on Christ the iniquity of us all and treated Him as a sinner, even though Christ never sinned Himself and then delivered Him up to

His death for our sake. Jesus died because of our sins, and we died in the Person of our Substitute. He arose from the dead, having in Himself the life He was to give to His followers. Christ is 'the Righteousness of God,' and those who really get Christ get this Righteousness.

We have spoken of how we were all made dead, spiritually, by Adam's sin. This sin separated us from God, but He did not want this to be the end of man and He had a plan for man to be in right standing with Him once more. This plan was in Jesus Christ to come and take the sins of the world upon Himself so that we may be made whole again, as we have already seen. Paul shows us this again in Romans.

> **"For if by the one man's offense death reigned through the one, much more those who receive abundance of grace and the gift of righteousness will reign in life through the One, Jesus Christ. Therefore, as through one man's offense judgement came to all men, resulting in condemnation even so through one Man's righteous act the free gift came to all men, resulting in justification of life. For as by one man's disobedience many were made sinners, so also by one Man's obedience many will be made righteous." Romans 5:17-19 NKJV**

We <u>have</u> been made the righteousness of God through Him as Paul shows us in verse 21 of 2 Corinthians, chapter 5. So, are we as righteous and accepted, in the eyes of God, as Jesus Christ? You bet we are!! Praise God that he has given His grace to us. It is not because of anything that we have done or could ever do to receive this grace. It is <u>**only**</u> by what **He has already done for us**. We could never earn the grace He has given, as a free gift, to us.

# Chapter 21

# *MORE THAN CONQUERORS*

● ● ● ● ● ● ● ● ● ● ● ● ● ● ● ● ● ● ● ●

*When there seems no way out...Let God In!*

Have you ever had a situation or problem that you wanted to overcome or conquer? Maybe it is smoking, drinking or maybe it's drugs. Perhaps it is the need to "shop 'till you drop" or maybe even it is just to succeed in school or work. Did you know that **IN CHRIST**, you can be a conqueror; you can overcome any situation you may encounter; you can have the victory over anything that is controlling you.

These words tend to inter-relate to each other within the Greek language. Let's look at their definitions so we can understand their use within the Scriptures. First, we have "Conquer", taken from the Greek word, 'nikao', meaning "to overcome" (its usual meaning), is translated "conquering" and "to conquer."[1] Second is, "Overcome", which also is taken from 'nikao' translated to be used (a) of God, (b) of Christ and (c) of His followers meaning, "mightiest prevail".[2] And last is "Victorious", which again, comes from 'nikao', here meaning, "to conquer, overcome".[3] Now that we have the definitions down, let us look at what the Word says. The first verse we will look at is I John 2:13:

> **"I write to you, fathers, because ye have
> known Him Who is from the beginning. I write
> to you, young men, because ye have con-
> quered the evil one..." (ASW)**

John tells us here that we have already conquered Satan because we are **IN CHRIST** and goes on to tell us in a later verse that we have done this because He is in us.

> "You are of God, little children, and have <u>over-</u>
> <u>come</u> them, because He who is in you is
> greater than he who is in the world."
>
> 1 John 4:4 (NKJV)

It is our faith **IN CHRIST** that makes us able to overcome in this life. This is shown to us in 1 John 5:4.

> "For whatever is born of God <u>overcomes</u> the
> world. And this is the <u>victory</u> that has <u>over-</u>
> <u>come</u> the world - our faith.  (NKJV)

Paul confirms this victory we have through Christ in Corinthians.

> "But thanks be to God, who gives us the vic-
> tory through our Lord Jesus Christ."
>
> 1 Corinthians 15:57 (NKJV)

Not only are we conquerors, overcomers and victors; we are "more than conquerors", as Paul states in Romans.

> "Yet in all these things we are more than con-
> querors through Him who loved us"
>
> Romans 8:37

Worrell says, "we gain more through Christ than we lost in Adam." The believer, who has Christ enthroned in his heart, should be better, the stronger, for every battle; and the better equipped for future conflicts. With Christ, there is <u>nothing</u> that you cannot overcome. The Bible says, **"I can do <u>all things</u> through Christ who strengthens me"** (Phil 4:13).

---

[1] Vine's, (p 122)
[2] Vine's, (p 453)
[3] Vine's, (p 660)

# Chapter 22

# *WHERE YOUR IDENTITY LIES*

• • • • • • • • • • • • • • • • • • •

*"For the message of the cross is foolishness*
*to those who are perishing, but to us who are*
*being saved it is the power of God."*
*1 Corinthians 1:18 (NKJV)*

A knowledge of the believer's identity **IN CHRIST** is the rock
or building block of the Christian life. You have to know who you
are and that you are accepted, as you are, by God to be able to
grow in your relationship with Him. Please note, I said to be able
to <u>GROW</u> in your <u>RELATIONSHIP WITH HIM</u>. It has nothing to
do with your receiving salvation from Him. You can not live the
Christian life; you can not imitate Christ. Only Christ can. It has
to be Him living within you for you to overcome.

It is only through learning and trusting in our identity as it is
taught in the Bible that we become free from the false identities
that the world gives to us. Whatever you depend upon in life for
your identity i.e. drugs, money, jobs, or other material possessions, etc., that is what will control you. Once you learn that
Christ is what you need, then that need for Him will control you
and you have your true identity. When you learn from His Word
that you are accepted by Him, as you are, then you can start to
accept and love others as they are. None of us are perfect and
we never will be as long as we are on earth. We can be as perfect as possible with Christ in us and living through us in our daily
walk. We have to know that our acceptance is not based on what
we are doing, but on the perfection of Christ that has been done
for us. We have <u>total</u> acceptance **IN CHRIST!**

Where is your identity? Is it in what you do, what you own or is it in Christ? If in Christ, you do not have to worry with impressing others with possessions. Christ is there for you if <u>YOU</u> will only let Him in. For He said:

> **"Behold, I stand at the door, and knock: If <u>any</u> man hear my voice, and open the door, I will come in..." Revelation 3:20**

When you were born again, you were not half-reborn, you were not made half-righteous. You were made **the righteousness** of God **IN CHRIST**. You are a joint-heir with Him. A joint-heir refers to a personal equality based on a equality of possession. Jesus went to the Cross to give you what He already possessed. He arose so you could be recreated in His image. You are more than a conqueror **IN CHRIST**.

It is **IN CHRIST, IN HIM, or IN WHOM** that this is possible, but what do these terms mean? Can we just say we are IN HIM and have everything? NO! We have discussed this in part, but let's look somewhat deeper at this.

Too many people read these verses with **In Him, In Christ, or In Whom,** yet they fail to realize just what this means. It was not until I saw a film produced by Campus Crusade for Christ called, "JESUS" that I came to a full understanding of this myself. For the first time in my life, I realized what Christ went through for me, even before I was born, and this is something we all need to understand.

Upon being convicted, not once, but three times, Jesus was given a Roman flogging, which was nothing less than a brutal beating. He was stripped, possibly tied to a post, and beaten on the back with an instrument made of short, leather whips studded with sharp pieces of bone or metal. This alone could have been fatal. After this, He was taken into the courtyard where some 200-300 soldiers repeatedly struck Him with a staff and spat on Him to humiliate Him. At this point, He was taken to the cruelest form of death known to man; crucifixion.

This man had been beaten to a bloody pulp, barely able to walk of His own power, and so weak that a stranger, Simon of

Cyrene, was made to carry the crossbar from which Jesus was to later hang and Christ did this for me.

Laid on the ground with outstretched arms, He was nailed to the cross then lifted to the beam where His feet were nailed as well. Death was usually slow, very painful and known to take as long as three days to die. He was offered a drink of wine mixed with myrrh, a plant's sap having the effects of anesthetic, to offer relief from the pain, but He declined so He could remain in control of Himself.

To be **IN CHRIST**, we have to die with Him. We have to accept the flogging He received; we have to be nailed to that cross as He was and we have to feel the pain He felt. When Christ died, we died. But like Him, we arose with a new life through Him. This is to be **IN CHRIST!!** Just saying we are **IN CHRIST** or **IN HIM** is not enough. We must realize what Christ went through for us and accept it as our own. He took it all upon Himself for the world, for us, and we must accept and receive what He did for us to be **IN HIM.**

When you accept that, your life will never be the same. You will grow in the Lord and accept the position of authority He has given you and you will take your rightful place beside Him. As His people, we are everything to God that Jesus is.

He is there for you. Do you dare to open the door to Him? Do you want that joy, peace, happiness, forgiveness, and righteousness of God? Only Christ can give it to you. You will not find it in drugs, sex, alcohol, cars, money, jobs, or anything you might possess. You will only find it **IN CHRIST.** Are you ready to accept the pain He suffered for you? Have you died and then been made alive? **IN CHRIST,** you are somebody. Who are you?

Following this chapter, you will find a plan of salvation, if you have never accepted Christ into your life, and a version of the "sinner's prayer." These words, in and of themselves, do not have the power to save you. It is the sincere desire in your heart that makes the difference and that is what God is looking for.

If you want Christ in your life and you are sincere, then follow this plan and pray the prayer of salvation to receive Christ into your life. Then find a good Bible church and become active in it to continue your growth...**IN CHRIST.**

## Plan of Salvation

1) We must all realize we are sinners.

   **"For all have sinned and come short of the glory of God."**
   **Romans 3:23**

2) We must understand that because of sin, we die.

   **"For the wages of sin is death; but the gift of God is eternal life through Jesus Christ our Lord." Romans 6:23**

3) God said if we will but come to Him, He will not cast us out.

   **"All that the Father giveth me shall come to me; and him that cometh to me I will in no wise cast out." John 6:37**

4) We must confess with words, Jesus is Lord and call upon His name to be saved from death. We must also believe in our hearts for our salvation.

   **"That if thou shall confess with thy mouth the Lord Jesus and shall believe in thine heart that God raised him from the dead, thou shall be saved. For with the heart man believeth unto righteousness; and with the mouth confession is made unto salvation. For whosoever shall call upon the name of the Lord shall be saved."**
   **Romans 10:9-10, 13**

Dear Heavenly Father,
I realize I am a sinner and I confess and repent of all my sins, past and present. Your Word says if I will come to you, You won't cast me out, but You will take me in. I come to you now, Father. I stand on your Word, and confess Jesus Christ is Lord and the Son of God. I believe He was raised from the dead to save me from my sins. I am calling on His name, so I know that You now save me. I believe with my heart and I confess Jesus as my Lord and Savior. I am saved!!! Thank you, Father, for your wonderful gift of salvation!! Amen.

# *Author's Note*

"I can do all things in Christ which strengtheneth
me...because greater is he that is in you, than he
that is in the world."
Philippians 4:13 & 1 John 4:4

# Author's Note

This book was written with teenagers and young adults in mind, but it is not limited to them, by any means. It is my prayer that by sharing my life with you; by showing you the mistakes I made in life; and how, by placing my identity in material possessions was incorrect, that it will, in some way, prevent you from making the mistakes I have in life. By helping to keep your family together, friendships alive, and by showing you the way to have complete happiness and joy in your life, right now, is my desire and prayer.

If but one boy, girl, man or woman is kept from behind prisons walls, physical and/or mental; to lead one person to Jesus Christ as their personal savior, then all of my suffering, pain, and years behind bars will have been worth it.

There are many, many additional Scriptures in the Bible that cover the topics we have covered in this writing. These are just the ones selected for our purpose of illustration. I pray you will do an even deeper study, on your own, and let the Holy Spirit guide, direct, and reveal to you the other verses that will help you in your personal walk and growth with the Lord.

Just remember to keep Jesus Christ first and foremost, in every area of your life.

In His love & Mine,

Alan

**GUILTY AS CHARGED**

# *Appendix*

"If we live, we live to the Lord, and if we die, we die to the Lord. So then, whether we live or we die, we belong to the Lord. So let us then definitely aim for and eagerly pursue what makes for harmony and for mutual upbuilding of one another." Romans 14:8,19 (Amp.)

# *"THOUGHTS AFTER TWO YEARS GONE"*

Time is infinite and creeps on knees
made stiff with age — so slowly does it crawl;
But looking back, the years have flown,
each so useless — each a void.

Perhaps it is this that makes it so,
the painfully slow, yet rapid flight,
of many days, none with a face, none with its mark;
one like another in long endless procession.

What fate is it that holds us so,
suspended in this abhorrent void;
surrounded close by an alien force,
while all around us life flows on.

I seek the light that issues forth,
from that which I know and those whom I love;
that which now seems like a dream from the past,
and forms my greatest hope for the future.

With faith and hope, I will survive,
determined not to falter, not to die;
a promise to myself to stay alive,
swearing that to oneself, one cannot lie.

So, infinite time, creep on, creep on;
or speed like Mercury, as the wind;
for though suspended, imprisoned, bound,
my mind reaches out to touch the light.

And somewhere in the surrounding dark;
the light I seek already glows;
perhaps from here 'tis only a glimmer,
but at the source, it is sunbright and strong.

**GUILTY AS CHARGED**

So I will span the time between,
and at time's end I'll touch the light;
for I have felt the Lord's strong hand,
and with His help, I cannot fail.

10/04/90

# "WHAT YOU HAVE DONE"

When will this world see
There is a light shining in Thee.

That fills the soul to over flowing
and sooths the sorrows that are looming.

I long for the day when the fresh world begins,
when life's struggles will be a memory dim.

When the light of glory shall fill our eyes
and love and joy shall know the depths of our lives.

You died to give us life -
You died to end our strife -

If only the world would see
What you have done for me.

07/91

# *"DWELL DEEP, DWELL HIGH"*

Go study the stars and then see thy true stature,
Go walk by the sea thy real value to learn;
Breath deep, the sweet scent of the Lebanon Cedars,
And henceforth all meanness and pettiness spurn.

Reach up to the sky, then, in fond aspiration,
Encompass all heaven in credo and plan;
'Tis only when man dares to dare in his reaching,
That life deigns to notice and value the man.

Man's life is not spanned by the years that flit by him,
Nor progress full-meted and measured in miles;
The reach of his soul and the scope of his love,
His struggles, his battles against Satan's wiles -

These mark out the man as they weed out the weakling,
These tag a real man with his value and worth;
For Heaven's a cinder, eternity empty,
Unless man can find timeless values on earth.

08/91

# "MY WILL BE DONE?"

I asked the Lord to make all my dreams come true,
and settled back to wait for what He did not do.

I asked Him to change my limited circumstances,
then waited in vain for improvements in finances.

I asked Him to heal me of a nagging disability,
but all He did then was to ignore me.

Desperately I sought Him, asking nothing now,
except to serve Him, for Him to teach me how.

I pled just for Him in deep humility.
Then He did change things, He changed me!

07/92

I have, on many occasions, had troublesome feelings or needed help in which I have turned to God's Word for help. I have listed some of the areas I had trouble with and the Scriptures that helped me in each case. Perhaps they will help you as well.

**Afraid:**  Psalms 91; Hebrews 13:5-6; 1 John 4:13-18

**Anxious:**  Matthew 6:24-34; 1 Peter 5:7

**Depressed:**  Psalms 23, 130; John 3:16-17; Ephesians 3:14-21

**Discovering God's Will:**  Matthew 5:14-16; Luke 9:21-27; Romans 13:8-14; 1 John 4:7-21

**Death of a friend/loved one:**  John 11:25-26; Romans 14:7-9; 1 Thessalonians 4:13-18

**Facing imprisonment:**  Matthew 25:31-46

**Facing a trial:**  Psalms 26; Matthew 5:25-26; Luke 18:1-8

**Impatient:**  Psalms 13, 37:1-7; James 5:7-11

**Lonely:**  Psalms 22; John 14:15-27

**Losing your job:**  Philippians 4:10-13

**Rejected:**  Psalms 38; Matthew 9:9-13; John 15:18-16:4; Ephesians 1:3-14

**Seeking forgiveness:**  Proverbs 28:13; Matthew 6:14-15; Hebrews 4:12-16; 1 John 1:5-10

**Tempted by sex:**  1 Corinthians 6:9-20; Galations 5:16-26

**Useless/inferior feelings:**  Ephesians 4:1-16; 1 Peter 2:4-10

There are many more verses that apply to these topics, and any other "trouble area" you may have. I pray you will take the time to study God's Word and let the Word and the Holy Spirit guide and minister to you on a personal level.